Bo

Ahead … s.
They … n.

Leav… the young woman under the dinosaur spine of a
roller coaster, he crept forward until the men were in shot.
He shouldered the HK and slipped the Tekna from its sheath.
The three were too preoccupied to notice him…until it was
too late.

Bolan took out the man nearest him with a punch to the throat.
The soldier moved toward the second man, following up his
punch to the first with a stamp that crushed the guy's nose
and cheekbone. Bolan lunged and thrust upward, driving the
Tekna under the second guy's ribs. As the man fell, the soldier
turned, pulling the knife out.

The third man sprinted away. Bolan began to follow, but
instinct held him back. The acolyte ran over a rumpled
tarpaulin, and his foot caught a loop of wire and loosened
a stake that scythed between two huts, its arc vicious and
true. The point caught the man at neck level, slicing his head
from his body, which continued forward for two steps before
collapsing across the boardwalk.

Bolan could do nothing as the stake hit a metal strut with
a resounding clang, splinters of thick wood flying. Bolan
winced as a chunk of wood sliced into his thigh. He cursed as
he pulled it out.

He looked down at the wood in his hand and cursed again.
Even in the shadows he could see that one end of the long
splinter was stained darker. If he was lucky, the stain was his
own blood. If not, then he had a real problem.

MACK BOLAN ®

The Executioner

THE EXECUTIONER
DON PENDLETON'S
SLAYGROUND

A GOLD EAGLE BOOK FROM
WORLDWIDE®

TORONTO • NEW YORK • LONDON
AMSTERDAM • PARIS • SYDNEY • HAMBURG
STOCKHOLM • ATHENS • TOKYO • MILAN
MADRID • WARSAW • BUDAPEST • AUCKLAND

Recycling programs
for this product may
not exist in your area.

First edition November 2014

ISBN-13: 978-0-373-64432-2

Special thanks and acknowledgment to
Andy Boot for his contribution to this work.

Slayground

Power that is acquired by violence is only usurpation and only lasts as long as the force of the individual who commands can prevail over the force of those who obey.
—Denis Diderot
from *The Encyclopedia of Diderot and d'Alembert*

Whether the violence is physical or psychological, it is my duty to take down those who seek to exploit and control people weaker than themselves.
—Mack Bolan

THE
MACK BOLAN
LEGEND

Nothing less than a war could have fashioned the destiny of the man called Mack Bolan. Bolan earned the Executioner title in the jungle hell of Vietnam.

But this soldier also wore another name—Sergeant Mercy. He was so tagged because of the compassion he showed to wounded comrades-in-arms and Vietnamese civilians.

Mack Bolan's second tour of duty ended prematurely when he was given emergency leave to return home and bury his family, victims of the Mob. Then he declared a one-man war against the Mafia.

He confronted the Families head-on from coast to coast, and soon a hope of victory began to appear. But Bolan had broken society's every rule. That same society started gunning for this elusive warrior—to no avail.

So Bolan was offered amnesty to work within the system against terrorism. This time, as an employee of Uncle Sam, Bolan became Colonel John Phoenix. With a command center at Stony Man Farm in Virginia, he and his new allies—Able Team and Phoenix Force—waged relentless war on a new adversary: the KGB.

But when his one true love, April Rose, died at the hands of the Soviet terror machine, Bolan severed all ties with Establishment authority.

Now, after a lengthy lone-wolf struggle and much soul-searching, the Executioner has agreed to enter an "arm's-length" alliance with his government once more, reserving the right to pursue personal missions in his Everlasting War.

1

"Do as I say and no one will get hurt. Don't, and maybe you will." The words were followed by a vulpine grin that suggested the speaker would love someone to step out of line so he could show he meant what he said.

It didn't look as if he was going to get the opportunity. Inside the Griffintown branch of the Florida First State Bank, everyone had hit the floor. It was a small space, between the half-frosted glass wall facing the street and the main counter. The lines to the tellers were cramped by tables for deposit slips. There had been two tellers on duty, five customers, and an aging security guard who had been slow on the uptake and due to retire in three weeks. If the pool of blood soaking the carpet around his head was anything to go by, he wasn't likely to make retirement.

Thursday afternoon, and the two mothers with babies, the hardware store clerk depositing takings, and the two men waiting to withdraw cash and cursing the defective ATM had been shocked for a frozen moment by the four people who had slipped in and bolted the double doors. A man and a woman stood at the front windows, the woman nervously peering out, then rapidly glancing back to the interior, the man coolly training his Glock machine pistol on the floor. The woman carried a mini-Uzi. Anyone who looked carefully enough would see it gently shaking.

The vulpine man, whose bearing and speech marked him as the alpha male, had strode into the middle of the room, whipping an HK MP5 from beneath his duster and waving it in an arc, the implicit threat enough to make the customers and tellers snap out of their fear freeze and hit the deck. The woman who had joined him was stone-faced, her eyes unreadable, but leaving little doubt as to her intent.

The vulpine man looked up to one of the closed-circuit television cameras that surveyed the bank interior from all angles.

"An audience. Good. I want you to listen. We do not want to harm these people, but if they get in our way, they are expendable. Make no doubt of that. Today's little raid is to help finance our crusade against the state that seeks to oppress us and to force us ever closer to extinction. We have inside knowledge of the way in which our government—which has the audacity to claim that it serves on our behalf—is working, and we will bring it to its knees. As you can see, we have Elena Anders, who is a devotee of the Seven Stars, and who is committed to our cause. Through her, we have discovered more of the secrets of power. When the time is right, and we can launch our revolution of the heart and mind, her knowledge will be shared with more than just our existing brethren. Then the fire of justice can spread throughout the land, and we will be as free as our constitution promises we are."

The woman murmured something too low for the mics on the CCTV to pick up clearly. The alpha man shot her a venomous glance, but nodded briefly in deference to her and turned to the tellers.

"You—out here, now. Don't give me no time-lock shit, either. The locks you have on the vaults here have manual overrides. I want you and everyone in the back room out here now. Call the sheriff and it's the babies who'll get it first. You want that on your piggy little consciences?"

To emphasize his point, he fired a short burst into the floor between the two mothers, who screamed hysterically as they clutched their children to them.

It had the desired effect: within a couple minutes, bank bags with cash, securities and items from safe deposit had been piled on the counter, ready to be carried out. The vulpine man's psychology had been sound; this was a small town where everyone was either distantly related or friends of friends. There were no strangers here, and no one wanted anyone to get hurt. They complied almost with eagerness.

He gestured to his stone-faced companion and to the nervous woman by the door. They moved forward and loaded the haul into large hemp sacks, which they then carried toward the doors as their compatriot undid the bolts. The vulpine man covered their retreat, pausing before he exited to stare directly at the camera above the door. His smile this time was arrogant and triumphant before he moved out of frame.

The footage continued for a few minutes after this. The people in the bank were too shocked to move or make a sound for a few eerie seconds. In the distance, the sirens of a late-arriving cruiser approached. The raiders' research and preparation had been good—they'd picked a time when the sheriff's staff roster was low, and they'd placed hoax calls that stretched the department's resources, dragging officers far from the main street and buying valuable time.

Then, just before the CCTV footage finally elapsed, the silence was broken by a wail of fear and relief from one of the mothers. After that, pandemonium broke out, as the hardware clerk and one of the men rushed to offer what first aid they could to the stricken security guard, while the bank staff and the other male customer tried to comfort the mothers and children.

The picture cut out abruptly just as the sheriff's team entered the bank.

Hal Brognola hit the remote, and the wide-screen monitor on which they had been viewing the footage blinked and shut off.

"What about the guard?" Mack Bolan asked, although he was certain he already knew what the big Fed would say.

"Three days in intensive care. Didn't regain consciousness," he said shortly, shaking his head. "Albert Myres, sixty-year-old vet. Fifteen years on the Jacksonville sheriff's department, twenty-five in the service."

"Some part-time job for retirement," the soldier said. His tone was brooding, both at the waste of the old man's life, and the stupidity of the suits who had thought nothing of putting him in that position.

Brognola shrugged. "People walk around with their eyes shut all the time, Striker. Not much we can do about that. And to be fair, this is a real sleepy town where nothing much happens aside from the annual gator hunt. It's a family and retirement town, with just the newspaper industry to keep it afloat."

Bolan frowned. "Newspapers? In rural Florida?"

"I use the term loosely." Brognola shrugged. "It's the editorial and printing headquarters for the *Midnight Examiner*. Hardly cutting edge news, but—"

"But it's been a while since I was in line at the supermarket long enough to be tempted," Bolan finished. "I had no idea that rag was still going."

"It's not what it was, but it keeps the town afloat. More relevant to us, it still has a strong circulation, and being the only game in town, it got to the CCTV before we did."

Bolan's eyebrow quirked. "*We*, Hal? Why would a small-town robbery interest you that much?"

"You heard the man on the movie. Elena Anders."

As he spoke, Brognola tossed a copy of the *Midnight Examiner* across the desk. Bolan picked it up and scanned the headlines. "But there's nothing in here about any bank robberies."

"Exactly," Brognola said.

As Bolan read on, it became obvious that the *Midnight Examiner's* reputation as a celebrity scandal sheet and paranormal purveyor left its writers ill-equipped to cover the kind of story that had fallen into their laps.

"The Seven Stars is a religious cult," Brognola explained. "They peddle a mix of Christianity and an apocalyptic worldview fueled by too many B-movies and 'true-life' UFO books. A few months ago, Senator Dale Anders's daughter, Elena, left her college in Tampa and fell in with this cult. Our intel stops there. At this point, we can only speculate about how much of Ms. Anders's participation is willing, and how much of it is forced."

Bolan sighed as he threw down the tabloid. "They clearly excel in stories about celebrity diets and alien abductions, but why would they omit such a huge scoop? Especially if they got the footage?" He paused. "There's a backstory here, right? And it won't be long before the serious reporters start sniffing around."

Brognola nodded, but remained silent.

"There's a reason this hasn't broken yet," Bolan continued. "And there's a reason you called me here."

Brognola walked across the room and stared out his office window.

"Dale Anders is a good man, Striker. A kind, fair man. That's rare enough among senators, these days. He's the kind of guy Jimmy Stewart would have played."

"We're not doing this—whatever this is—because you like him, Hal," Bolan said softly.

The big Fed shook his head. "No, but it is relevant. Dale really cares about his job. He's never courted headlines, and doesn't see this as a fast track to presidential nomination. He actually wants to make a difference. Both sides of the House like him, despite policy differences. He's got integrity. I know he was worried about

Elena for a good while before she finally disappeared. He even tried to accept that she was old enough to make her own decisions, even though it killed him. But anyone with half a brain gets alarm bells ringing when it comes to crank cults, and so he called me up for some advice, and maybe some information. He'd been trying to establish some kind of communication with her for several months, and I'd kept the press at bay for him. We both hoped this could be resolved without any undue attention."

"Not much chance of that now," Bolan said quietly.

"This is the third raid in as many weeks," Brognola said. "That's a hell of a lot. They're either trying to grab as much as possible before the law catches up with them, or else they desperately need the cash. And if that's the case, then you've got to wonder why. Just what do they have planned?"

"So what *do* you know about them?"

"The asshole with the HK who loves the camera is Duane Johansen. Thirty-four, served ten years on a robbery charge. Files show that there were probably a whole lot more that he didn't get arraigned for because of lack of evidence."

"These cults will take anyone these days. Other IDs?"

"Not on this raid. The woman standing next to Johansen is on all three, but she hasn't been identified. On the second raid they had a crystal meth dealer named Arnie Fry, who's dabbled in illegal arms on a small scale."

"So they know what they're doing. At least, some of them do. What about the rest of the cult?"

"The Seven Stars. When they align it will be a sign that the time of great change is on us, blah-blah-blah. The usual." Hal waved dismissively. "There's a file on them that I can get Bear to download for you. It's not pretty reading. The usual collection of misfits, criminals and the confused."

Bolan nodded. "I get your point, but it could be dangerous to think of them that simply. These raids seem to have been pretty well planned and executed. If they can do that…"

"I know," Brognola agreed, rubbing his forehead.

"Well, what would make her—or them—a target?" Bolan asked.

Brognola smiled wryly. "On the money, Striker. Dale is a very conscientious man. He serves on committees that deal with the procurement and deployment of software and hardware that are vital to homeland security. A lot of very sensitive information passes through his hands."

"Blackmail, then?"

"It doesn't have to be that crude. We're pretty sure that the Seven Stars have put two and two together, and it won't be long before other enemies of the homeland do so when more information leaks."

"What kind of information?"

"Elena was a good student before the cult started to get to her. She was like her father—very studious, very conscientious, very hardworking…and very patriotic. College vacations weren't a holiday for her."

Bolan assented. "I think I see where you're going.

Not being one for spring break, Elena liked to busy herself helping her father, right?"

Brognola agreed. "She was an additional secretary and researcher, which meant she had access to a lot of sensitive information. Also, her mother died two years ago, so Elena became her father's confidante when it came to his work."

"I can see why you wanted to keep a lid on this, and why you're keen to get her back. But if she had that much access, where the hell was security when they should have been keeping an eye on her?"

"Slipped through the net, Striker. She was never on payroll or official staff. Only Dale really knew how much she was privy to, and that was why he came to me. Make no mistake, this is a sensitive issue."

Bolan's tone was grim. "If you have too many agencies involved, crawling over half of Florida, then you alert everyone, from the press to our enemies, that Elena Anders is more than just a runaway daughter. If you leave it to the local boys on the ground, then you're looking at Waco and a bad result for the senator personally. In between the two, there's no knowing what these whack-jobs have got out of her and what they'll do with it."

"That's about the size of it. Elena was at Tampa, but since hooking up with the cult she's moved farther south…."

"I gathered that." Bolan stood and walked across the room to where a map of the United States covered half of one wall. He reached out and indicated the southern Florida area, around the Keys. "If what just hap-

pened here—" he drew a circle with his finger "—and
the other two robberies took place within a radius like
this, then it figures that the cult is based somewhere
within the circle, which would put it right in the swamplands—tough to access without drawing a whole lot of
unwanted attention to yourself."

Brognola nodded. "We know where they are. They
make no secret of that. The problem is it's not exactly
easy to get to." He stepped in front of Bolan and indicated a spot almost in the exact center of the circle the
soldier had traced. "There's an abandoned amusement
park that was built in the seventies. Eveland. As in Evel
Knieval rather than Adam and Eve. All the rides and
attractions were themed around the old rider's stunts."

"Should have made a killing back then," Bolan
mused. "And he's become almost mythical since dying,
so why is it a wreck?"

Brognola grinned. "Money. First of all, they ne-
glected to give old Evel any for using his name and
image. And even if they'd done that, or won the result-
ing court case, they were too mean to grease the right
palms when it came to getting an interstate re-routed so
that it passed nice and close to where they were situated.
As a result, it's been closed for thirty years, a hunk of
useless real estate accessible only by one or two small
roads that wind through the tropics."

"Not good for whoever was fool enough to put money
in, but more than good enough for this cult's purposes,"
Bolan mused. "So what's needed is a small force—
maybe just one man—who can move quickly and without detection, to extract the Senator's daughter. Once

she's safe, then that small force can blow them out of the water. That's if that doesn't happen during the extraction itself. And that one man would be me, or why else would I be here? Am I right?"

Brognola clapped him on the shoulder. "Striker, you are so on the money today that I'm tempted to send you to the racetracks en route."

2

Elena Anders felt her breath catch as a sob rose in her throat. She tried to choke it back. Her heart was thudding so loudly that she was sure they could hear it as far away as Miami. Her clothes—ripped denim cutoffs and a soiled T-shirt—were clinging to her. She was dripping with sweat, yet her mouth felt as dry as a desert. Her ears were ringing and her head was thumping with the effort she had put in so far, and she could feel the lactic acid burning in her muscles, sapping them of strength as she tried to loosen the paling that was driven deep into the soil, supporting the wire fence. All the while, she was glancing nervously around, the tension and anxiety doing nothing for her aching head. Thoughts that were already a whirl of confusion became even more jumbled, making it an effort to concentrate on the task at hand.

Somewhere in the back of her mind, that part of the distant consciousness that was still able to attain any kind of clarity, she was sure that they were doping her up. She was pretty sure, in fact, that everyone in the compound was getting drugged, in varying degrees. She thought of the area as a compound, like a penitentiary, even though it was supposed to be a commune. Maybe it was someone's idea of a commune, but it certainly wasn't hers. Nothing about the Sanctuary of the Seven Stars had been how she had imagined it when they'd ensnared her in Tampa.

Ensnared. Again, that wasn't what some would call it. Back then, she probably would have agreed with them....

Dammit, Elena, focus, she told herself. It was only by some miracle that she'd been able to slip away from the others. A chance like this wouldn't come around again in a hurry, so she had to make the most of it.

She braced herself and pushed, so that the paling moved in a circular pattern, carving out a larger hole. Biting through her lip until she could taste the salt of blood, and feel at least a little moisture on her parched tongue, she used the pain to drive her beyond what she thought herself capable of. She gripped the paling, pulled it to her and heaved upward. Despite herself, the effort caused a gasp of pain to escape her bloody lips.

It was done. She staggered under the weight of the picket, letting it fall away from her before it could swing in the other direction and crush her. It dropped with a dull thud, and for a moment she stood panting, listening hard and not quite able to believe that it hadn't created enough noise to draw anyone to the spot.

Elena forced herself into action. Every second mattered, as her absence could be noticed at any moment. She had to take advantage of this, even though her muscles protested and she felt as if she was moving through the swamp mud that she knew at some point she would have to face.

Where the paling had fallen, it had dragged the wire fencing out of shape, twisting it so that it was raised up from the scrub grass around the perimeter. It gave her a gap just big enough to crawl through. She fell onto her belly and dragged herself forward, ignoring the stones that scraped her stomach and knees, and the sharp ends of wire that snagged her T-shirt and the skin on her back and arms. The extra effort required to pull herself free was almost too much, but fear of what might happen if she was to be found like this, defenseless and with no chance of flight, was enough to spur her on. Finally, she pulled herself through to the other side.

Scrambling to her feet, she half stumbled and half ran into the cover of the thick undergrowth that threatened to encroach on the old theme park, and reclaim it for the Keys.

The main area used by the Seven Stars was on the far side of the park, where the entrance had once stood, the turnstiles now removed to make a large enough path for the cult's traffic. There were administration buildings and chalets that had been designed for workers, with a cafeteria and shower block that suited the group's communal lifestyle very well.

Farther into the park, where some of the rides had begun to crumble with age and disuse, the Seven Stars had converted several buildings into garages for the vehicles they had acquired. Farther back still, in the machine housing of some of the rides, was their armory. They used what had once been the operating booth for the park's central attraction—a series of motorcycles that took riders over and around rows of buses, like a signature Knievel jump—as a safe block for the spoils of their bank raids and other money-gathering activities. This left great swathes of the park unused.

The cult was small—twenty people permanently on site, with a handful of others making forays into the outside world—and they preferred to stay in close proximity to each other. Vast tracts of land lay derelict, the rides slowly being absorbed back into the landscape as the humid climate took its toll on the metal and wood, and tendrils of vegetation crept through the fence and across the cracked concrete. Cult members patrolled these areas, ostensibly to ensure that any outsiders wishing to spy or cause harm were kept at bay. Elena was inclined to think, after a while, that it was more to keep the cult members in.

But what mattered right now was that the patrols were generally conducted at night. Daytime watches were intermittent and mostly assigned when Duane got too much crystal meth in his system and his paranoia got out of control. He wasn't top banana, but sometimes he acted as if he was. Ricke called him the head of security, and what Ricke said was law in the compound.

It was Ricke who had got her hooked on the Seven Stars. When Elena was at Tampa, she had been determined to devote herself to study. Since her mother died, she had been driven to achieve what both her parents had wanted. The senator was never as demanding a parent as her mother had been, at least not overtly. His attitude was that people had to be motivated by their own inner will and drive, not by coercion. He would have been appalled if he had realized how close to nervous exhaustion she had driven herself, working constantly when she should have been enjoying all aspects of student life, and then returning home to diligently assist her father in his work.

That was where it had all started to go wrong for her. She had no doubt that the senator had the best of motives. But the information that he was privy to, and the kind of actions he would have to sanction should the need arise, made her blood run cold. It seemed so contrary to his nature to be able to sign off on acts of war. Now, removed from the hothouse pressures of her own making, she could see how her father could prioritize and keep a sense of perspective.

She could only wish that had been the case for her. She'd become too wrapped up in her own world, and could not see beyond the realpolitik of the papers she'd read when she was assisting her father. The documents painted a worldview that, for her, was unremittingly bleak, and she despaired of finding a way of life that offered her some hope.

So when a local organization hosted a series of lectures on alternate beliefs and phenomena, she'd grabbed at it eagerly, both as a means of escape and also as a possible pathway to answers.

Looking back, she knew she'd been incredibly vulnerable, and oblivious. Her devotion to her studies and to helping her dad had left her not exactly friendless, but certainly distanced from her peers. Added to this, her absorption into the world of imminent political disaster had left her in a depressed state she only now recognized. The first glimmers of light in the darkness would claim her.

Daniel Ricke had been in the right place at the right time—a tall, graying and soft-spoken man with an insistent tone and a slow-burning, intense charisma. When he spoke, Elena felt that he was talking to her and only her. His voice was melodious, the rhythms of his words drawing her into the meaning. He spoke of how man must make a choice to face the new age with the courage of love alone, leaving behind the material and the venal so he could lose the trappings that kept him in a perpetual state of conflict.

To someone who was trying to come to terms with the kinds of measures that her country would adopt in an emergency, and the kind of actions that would trigger these responses, what Ricke was saying made perfect sense. She'd told him so afterward, and he'd offered to send one of his people to speak with her further.

That was how she met Susan Winkler. She, too, spoke in an insistent manner, though her own voice burned with the fire of the acolyte and was animated in a way that belied her impassive face. Winkler spoke of Ricke's plans to build a series of communities across the USA, and then across the world—by eschewing the use of internet technology to communicate, and relying instead on the slower, more drawn out process of word of mouth. "The longer the seed takes to flower, the stronger the bloom," was his creed. Winkler came from a life that had been littered with petty crime and drug abuse; she'd been sent on the wrong path by the

influence of the world around her. Now she could see
the right way. She had the zealotry of the convert, and
the slightly unhinged air of the hard drug abuser. Elena,
lost in her own confusion, had not noticed this until it
was too late.

With Ricke's words drummed into her by Winkler,
Elena had left Tampa and journeyed to the southeast of
the state to join the community. The group was small
and hadn't yet expanded, but they had the power of
truth behind them.

"What…a…stupid…moron!" she gasped as she
stopped running. Her breath came in rasps that burned
at the pit of her stomach, and the humidity was making her sweat. She would have to find some fresh water
soon, or dehydration would cripple her. She could already feel her muscles cramping up.

She heard scuttling in the undergrowth, some crea-
ture hidden in the lush carpet of green that threatened
to trap her. The sun, directly overhead, was shaded by
a canopy of trees that left her in shadow. She had no
idea where she was headed. If she bore east from the
hole in the fence, she should be able to circle around
and come out on the rough road that led to the highway. She would have to hope she emerged far enough
away from the entrance to the old theme park that she
would not be seen.

They must know by now she was gone. Ever since
Duane had taken her on an expedition with them, forcing her to hold a gun and play a part in an armed robbery, she had been kept under close observation. She
wasn't sure why. It had taken her long enough to work

out any kind of escape, and she was completely unsure
of what to do next. She was unlikely to get away and
raise an alarm, leading the police to the compound. If
she was honest with herself, she was more likely to get
lost, have an accident and die alone out here. With a
sinking in her gut, she realized that this was the most
she could realistically hope for—and what was worse,
she would prefer it to being recaptured.

She tried to get her bearings, but all she could see
was semitropical swamp that would probably lead her
into water and quicksand, with a dense wall of wood
and vine before her, in which critters keen to bite her
face off certainly lurked. She would just have to guess,
hope for the best and press on. There was little else she
could do, and standing here waiting to be captured was
not on the list. She knew it was illogical, but movement
gave her hope.

She began to blunder through the undergrowth once
more, now heedless of the sounds she made as she
crashed through the vegetation, stumbling over roots
and slipping on mud and leaves. Her only goal was to
get as far from the compound as possible.

As she ran, her confrontation with Ricke came into
her mind. She had replayed it time and again since it had
happened. How had she been so stupid as to be taken
in by such a charlatan…? Or was he? Maybe he truly
believed in what he said, but was so stupid himself that
he couldn't see his own failure to strip himself of the
venality for which he castigated the entire human race.

Ricke lived in one chalet with the five women who
were his "wives." It had the best quality furniture, in-

cluding some antiques that he had acquired along the way, and a large collection of books that spilled untidily across the floor. The "wives" were his alone, whereas everyone else slept and shared communally in a kind of "free love" arrangement that had scared the hell out of Elena. Interestingly—given his preaching—Ricke used a tablet to keep in touch with the outside world, which Elena had noticed at their last meeting. Such things were forbidden to the rest of the community.

Once again, she had told him that she wanted no part of the robberies, that she had no wish to do anything other than leave in peace and say nothing to anyone about the compound. In part this was true, since she would rather no one knew how idiotic she'd been to be sucked in. But she could also see that Ricke was dangerous. Not on a grand scale, but certainly on a local one, especially with psychotics like Duane and Arnie as his right-hand men.

Ricke had sent his wives away when Elena had finished speaking. Only Arnie was left, lurking by the door and laughing softly to himself.

"Sweet child," Ricke had begun, in tones that made her shudder. "You have to understand that there are means to an end. These people in the outside world are so wrong and misled, and they don't understand us. It isn't their fault, but they would never cooperate unless we used the kind of language and behavior they understand. What we do is for the greater good."

"You can't seriously expect me to swallow that," she had replied, despite her instincts screaming out to keep her mouth zipped.

Ricke smiled, but not with his eyes, which stayed ice-cold and hard, penetrating into her. "I don't expect you to swallow anything, Elena. You came here because you believed. I think you still do. You just need to understand that our methods are justified by the results they obtain. It is all toward the greater good. Perhaps a period of quiet contemplation away from the others would help you realize this. I'm sure we can arrange that. And while you have this quiet time, you may do well to reflect on the things you've learned about our pig government from your father—a good man, I'm sure, but misguided. If we know what you know, we can use that to further the cause. Then there will be no need for the measures that, justifiably, cause you so much pain and anguish. Let Arnie show you where our cell of contemplation lies. And think carefully about what I have said to you...."

The softly giggling Arnie had led her out of the chalet and away from the main buildings to the place she had come to think of as a prison cell. And Elena had realized with an awful finality that the only way she would ever see the outside world again was if she escaped.

Thoughts of Ricke and her imprisonment were driven from her head as a black shape stepped out from behind the shelter of a tree and swung a lump of wood, catching her full in the solar plexus as she ran into it.

She retched, spitting out strings of bile, then looked up into the wolfish, leering face of Duane.

"Sugar, you didn't really think you could outrun me, did you?"

3

First stop for the soldier was a Miami naval base. Flown in by routine flight from Washington, he alighted and was greeted by the site's chief security officer, who showed him to a one-story block on the perimeter of the airfield.

Waiting for him, laid out on a table, was a driver's license, rental car registration, a billfold with cash and cards, a TEKNA knife and sheath, a Desert Eagle, gleaming and loaded with spare clips, and a shoulder holster. Sitting on a chair by the side of the desk was an attaché case with surveillance equipment including a monocular night vision headset, a camera and monitor with fiber-optic leads, and long-distance eavesdropping equipment with mic and receiver.

"I didn't know what kind of ordnance you required, Mr. Cooper, and as for a cell or tablet…well, I figured you'd probably be carrying your own. I can supply extra if you require."

Bolan nodded appreciatively. "No, that'll be fine, chief. You've done a great job, thanks. Did they give you any indication of why I'm here?"

The security man shook his head. "No, sir, and it's none of my damn business unless someone decides otherwise. The only thing I will say is that should the need arise, you just call in. Someone with your level of clearance has the privilege of telling me to jump, and how high."

"I don't think that'll be necessary, chief, but I appreciate the offer. As for the ordnance, I figure it's best for all concerned if I sort that out. No trails," he added cryptically. "There is one thing you could tell me, though."

"Just ask," the chief replied. He was in his late thirties, and had the deep tan of a man who had spent a long time around Miami and the Florida Keys. It was a good bet that he had the kind of local knowledge Bolan needed to tap.

"I'm heading over toward Griffintown, and I could use any on-the-ground intel that I won't pick up from regular background. You know the place?" The answer was obvious from the way the chief's eyebrows raised at the mention of the town, despite his attempts to keep a straight face.

"If I may say so, sir, it's a little off the beaten track for anything major to happen. Sleepy, small-town America—the kind of place they'd set some TV melodrama. The only thing that's happened there for the last fifty years was a recent bank robbery, where the guard was killed, and even that was supposed to be out-of-towners."

"Maybe, but isn't that kind of odd? All my other

intel points to the county being a swampland free-for-all. Moonshine and buckshot," Bolan added for effect.

"That's true enough, but you've got to remember that they've got the *Midnight* there. No one wants to end up on the front page, so they keep their noses clean. It's always been one of those tabloids that peddles morality, and as it's the main job provider, it doesn't pay to cross them. It helps that a lot of whackos are attracted to the area because of it, too. Guys who want to be abducted by little green men don't tend to be making moonshine," he added with a grin.

"That figures. Plenty of whackos around here, too, right? Cults and communes?"

"I hear there's one in an old amusement park, but they act like they're the Amish, you know? Keep to themselves and don't have much time for modern technology. They're harmless."

"That's good," Bolan said, keeping his voice level. Unless someone had reason to look below the surface, the Seven Stars must seem ineffectual from afar. But then, people had said that about Manson, his family and the Spahn Ranch half a century earlier.

For now, though, it was best that the security chief keep his illusions intact. Bolan thanked him and left the base, picking up the Ford sedan from the parking lot before heading out of Miami and into the less populated swamplands. Florida had one of the largest populations of any U.S. state, but the people were tightly packed into areas around the coast, such as Tampa and Miami, state capital Tallahassee and the largest single city, Jacksonville.

That gave Bolan pause for thought. Myres, the security guard who had been brutally struck down, had spent a long and distinguished term of service with the Jacksonville sheriff's department. Even at his age, he should have been ready for the quartet that had invaded the bank. The fact that they had taken him out so ruthlessly and efficiently suggested that they knew what they were doing, and that they were professional enough to have done their research. This gave the soldier two warnings: one, that they were not going to be caught out on their home turf that easily, and two, that they had sources of information in at least one town in the county. Either that or a source that could cover the whole county...a source such as the sheriff's office.

Bolan didn't want anyone to get a scent of who he was or why he was in the area. That meant the press, the Seven Stars themselves, and maybe even the local law enforcement.

Extract the target before her value—other than her human value—became a known commodity. Extract her with a minimum of disruption and consequent attention.

If he was going to do this, he would need more than just a handgun, and he knew where to get ordnance without raising questions or creating ripples in the swamp waters.

Bolan took the first turnoff on the road out of Miami, which would take him to Kendall. It was one of the smaller cities in the Miami metropolitan area, but it was still big enough to have more than its fair share

of criminal activity, and not so small that being there
would attract any undue attention.

Kendall had a number of housing projects and run-
down inner-city areas where businesses and homes had
gone to the wall, leaving gangs and street corner crime
in their wake. But it also had some areas of regeneration
that had sprung up before the double dip recession had
hit, and in these areas, entrepreneurs had made some
good out of the bad. Suburbs that were buoyed by these
pockets of cash still had manicured lawns and stucco
one-story haciendas with well-maintained pools. It was
into one of these areas that Bolan piloted his rented
Ford, pulling up before a house whose address he'd had
to check with Stony Man. It had been a long time, and
maybe his contact had moved. A large sum from one
of Bolan's war chests had also been wired into a bank
account connected to the cards he had picked up. He
would probably need it.

Leaving the sedan, Bolan walked across the lawn
and through the open side gate. He could hear laughter and voices from the backyard. Three teenage girls
in bikinis were frolicking in the pool, splashing each
other and laughing. A bony man with cropped graying
hair, clad in an orange robe, sat under an umbrella sip-
ping iced tea.

As Bolan approached, the man spoke without turning
around. "You'd better have an appointment, old chap.
If not, then a lawyer and a doctor, though maybe not
in that order."

"Knock knock," Bolan replied. "If I knew appoint-
ments were necessary these days, I would have called.

And you can tell your shadow he can drop the piece. If you still talk in those terms. A Glock semi, right? He'd better be accurate if he wants to be stupid, because I'll bet I'm quicker."

"Matt Cooper," the man murmured in an immaculate—if fake—British accent. "How nice to hear from you again. I always like returning customers, even if they do take several years to come back. Carl," he added in a louder voice, "do as the man says. He's not given to exaggerating. And please learn to be a little more discreet."

Bolan glanced over his shoulder. Through the open patio door he could see a man in a floral shirt and shorts lower his gun with a sour glance at the soldier. Bolan allowed himself a small grin. Nothing wrong with his peripheral vision.

"Don't be too hard on him, Yates," Bolan said. "Not many men would have noticed him there."

"It only takes one, dear boy," Yates said, languidly rising from his chair and turning to face the soldier. "You've worn well, I'll give you that. Better than I have. Better than anyone in our business has a right to."

"You're still alive," Bolan countered. "That's all that counts. And you're still pretending to be English."

"I am English. At least, my father was. I might have been born in Chicago, but my blood is that of the aristocracy, not the Mafia."

"I'll take your word for it." Bolan shrugged. "This is a pool party, is it?" he added, gesturing toward the girls.

"My daughter. Her mother was my maid. I think

she's back in Mexico now, though I really don't care. I like her friends to come over."

"That's sweet," Bolan said heavily. "Now, if you don't mind, much as I'd like to chew the fat, I'm here to do business."

"Of course." Yates gestured toward the house. Leaving the girls to continue splashing around, seemingly oblivious to the men's activities, Bolan went in through the patio doors.

Inside, the house was richly furnished in whites and creams, with splashes of purple from the drapes, rugs and cushions. It had a feminine touch.

"Carl, stop looking so pissed off and let Mr. Cooper through. He was always a good customer," Yates said in an almost prissy tone. From the way Carl deferred to him, with a barely concealed petulance, Bolan wondered how the hell the faux Englishman had ever managed to conceive a daughter.

"He doesn't look much like a Carl," Bolan remarked as they descended the stairs hidden by inset shelves. The walls were decorated with hangings depicting historical battles, and as they reached the basement he could see that the heavy oak desk and cases of weapons were more in keeping with the man as he knew him than the decor upstairs. A plasma-screen TV and a laptop were the only signs of the twenty-first century on display. A glass-fronted bookcase contained a large number of old books in lurid dust jackets.

"He isn't. That's just my little conceit. I call him Carl Petersen, just as I call myself Dornford Yates. The IRS call both of us something else completely. Or at least they would if they could find us."

"Touching, I'm sure. But that's none of my concern."

"Don't mind me, I just like to keep the personal touch," Yates murmured, leading Bolan through an aperture into the three connected rooms that housed the illegal ordnance that had paid for Yates's luxury.

Two things came to Bolan's mind as he followed. The first was that the supposed "personal touch" was an intriguing ruse. Yates was in a position to extract secrets from his customers that would no doubt be useful as leverage, or playing one buyer against the other. The second was more practical: Florida was one of the most waterlogged states in America. Although many richer homes had panic rooms and bunkers, shoring up a basement complex this large must have been expensive and disruptive. To do this unremarked spoke of Yates's ability to snake out tentacles of influence. Another time, and Bolan would maybe have to take him out of the game. But not now. There was other work to be done.

Bolan filled two duffel bags with grenades and plastic explosives, a Steyr and ammunition, a micro-Uzi with spare clips and an HK with the same. He had to balance the need for firepower with the need for speed and moving light. As he left the house with the bags, Carl shadowed him, to make sure he did so without delay. Bolan cast an eye toward the girls in the pool and wondered if they had any idea how their friend's father paid for all this—and whether they would even care if they did know.

Carl watched the soldier get into the sedan and pull

out. Bolan could see him in his rearview mirror as he turned off the quiet suburban street, and he felt a prickle at the back of his neck. Instinct was an inexact science, but it had kept him alive long enough for him not to ignore it.

AS THE SEDAN moved out of sight, Carl went into the backyard, closing the gate behind him. He called out to the girls to make sure they kept it shut, before moving back through the house and down to the basement. Yates was seated at his desk, staring into space.

"I don't like him," Carl said without preamble.

"We don't have to like them, we just have to like their money," Yates replied. "Frankly, I don't like any of them. But you're right about Cooper. Terrible name, obviously made up by some desk monkey with no imagination. No man who was completely in the fold would ever need to use a dealer like myself to supply his needs. However, someone who was working in such deep cover that they didn't officially exist…"

"If he's here to cause trouble, then chances are it's going to be with your customers," Carl said.

"Indeed," Yates said drily as he reached for the phone. "I don't mind setting them against each other if it makes me a profit, but someone like Cooper is not going to give me that kind of pleasure. If he's a government man of any stripe, then I think I may have a shrewd suspicion of where he's headed." As he spoke, he punched in a number.

"Ah, Ricke," he purred into the mouthpiece, "I think I have something that might be of interest to you.…"

No, no, Duane hasn't been causing any problems.... I don't know exactly what you're up to, but I think you should be aware of a few facts that have come to my attention...."

BOLAN TOOK A COUPLE hours to get away from the Miami metropolitan area and out into the county that was his destination. Once he crossed the border, he left the highways and took the smaller roads that led him to Griffintown. By the time he drove down the main drag it was dusk, and some of the larger stores were shut. The smaller mom-and-pop operations were still open, as were the diners and coffee shops. There was no mall on the outskirts of this town, so the streets were still busy. It looked idyllic.

At one end of the community was the small industrial park that housed the *Midnight Examiner*'s printing plant and editorial offices. Six stories tall, the building dwarfed everything else in town. In the evening light, it wasn't too fanciful to see how the town was dominated by the tabloid and its owners. How much they knew about the secretive cult on their stoop was something Bolan wanted to probe, if possible, without alerting an eager staff to a potential story.

Right now, he needed a hotel, a shower and a chance to study the rest of the intel Kurtzman had sent him, before getting some rest and checking out the area around Eveland.

He found a quiet hotel with a white-painted wooden facade, a terrace and a swing in the front yard. Inside, the owners had gone for the colonial look. A man who appeared to be the same age as the dead security guard, Myres, signed Bolan in. The ex-soldier and sheriff's officer should have been doing a job like this, not peddling his waning skills and waiting to be taken down. There was a lesson here, if Bolan cared to pay attention.

He was shown to his room, then thanked the proprietor, ordered a meal and took a shower. Over steak, Bolan studied the maps and topographic reliefs he'd downloaded. He had a fair idea of what to expect.

But there was nothing like the real thing.

4

Bolan left the hotel at sunrise. As this was a soft probe, he dressed in casual clothes rather than his blacksuit, although he wore combat boots for ease of movement on what might prove to be treacherous terrain. He had on a dark T-shirt and pants, with a loose jacket under which he carried the HK, plus spare magazines in his pants' pockets. The TEKNA knife was sheathed at the small of his back. In one of the duffel bags—the one not safely hidden with the rest of his ordnance back in his room—he carried the surveillance equipment, audio and visual, he'd picked up in Miami. He didn't foresee any real dangers at this stage, since he wasn't expected, as far as he was aware. Nonetheless, caution had to be balanced with traveling light and fast.

As he drove the sedan through Griffintown he saw very few signs of life—just a couple delivery trucks and a few people on their way to an early start at work. The monolith of the *Midnight Examiner* building loomed dark and brooding over the town.

Bolan was no reader of tabloids, but it did strike him as strange that the Seven Stars had never been

mentioned in the pages of the *Midnight Examiner*—
at least, not according to the background intel on the
group he had asked Stony Man to collate for him. To
have a loopy pseudo-religious cult in your backyard
would, he assumed, have been perfect for the tabloid's
agenda. It could be worth his while to find out if there
was a reason. Anything that might stand in the way of
his mission was worth a few minutes' detour. But right
now, there were more pressing matters.

The road before him was empty. Lush, tropical vegetation and low-lying trees hung over the edges of the
black ribbon of asphalt, threatening to take it back and
absorb it into the swamps and rich loam that lay beyond.

He traveled on for several miles until his GPS told
him he was approaching the old service road that cut
through to the derelict amusement park. He scanned the
sides of the highway for a spot where he could pull over
and take the sedan into some kind of cover.

About five hundred yards from the service road, he
noticed a semicircular patch of bare earth, likely formed
by vehicles repeatedly cutting into the vegetation. Bolan
figured it was likely to have been the sheriff's transport resting up or lying in wait for traffic violations.
He might as well take advantage; he didn't intend to be
long, and even if he encountered law enforcement because of this incursion, he could make use of the situation for further intel.

After pulling as far in as possible to shield the sedan
from casual view, Bolan got out and shouldered the
duffel bag, then took his bearings and headed into the
overgrown flora that bordered the blacktop. He would

probably be safe in that spot for a while, as it was still early and he had seen no traffic since leaving town. Evidently they were not believers in rising early in these parts.

The ground was soft, spongy with every step, and the roots and vines threatened to entangle his feet. There was no path, and he had to pick his way around tree trunks and thick brush. He could hear the scurrying of small animals as his approach scared them, the distant splashes as they ran through pools of water and mud in their bid to escape. Leaves in the canopy rustled as his progress disturbed birds nesting above his head. The constant background rattle and hum of insects made it hard for him to isolate any sounds that would indicate another human presence. If the senator's daughter was being kept captive against her will, then it was an outside possibility that the cult would have defensive patrols around their base. Come to that, given the nature of the cult, it was possible they would do so anyway. Their beliefs would incline them to paranoia.

Despite the early hour, the sun already bore down and the heat pulled humid puffs of steam from the soil. He could feel sweat start to prickle on his scalp and the small of his back.

Bolan pressed on, zigzagging as the vegetation dictated. He advanced half a mile through the dense undergrowth before he hit a sparser, more barren stretch. Through the filigree of leaves on bushes that sprouted along its length he could see the gap where the service road cut through the growth, leading to the old amusement park. The ground here was sodden, and it sucked at his boots. Having to almost pull his foot free with each step slowed him down, and he sought a slightly firmer footing. The muck explained why there was less growth along this edge, and also why the service road had been built up, to add a firmer base.

Cursing softly to himself, he moved back into the denser, harder-to-negotiate undergrowth. The road and the stretch running parallel to it would leave him too exposed, too close to the park entrance.

Circling out so he would reach Eveland's perimeter a good distance from the entrance, he stopped suddenly, senses quivering. Lurking beneath the sounds of the small animals and birds there was something else, something rhythmic and barely discernible. He was sure it was regular footfalls, now approaching him. He located the sound as coming from his right and about three hundred yards away. He was caught between what he must assume was an oncoming enemy and the edge of the park.

Bolan moved slowly forward, angling away from the footsteps. He kept low, using the bushes for cover. As the footfalls grew closer, he realized that there was more than one set. The rhythm was out of sync, an effect created by chance, and revealing that there were two people, one in pursuit of the other. Judging from the lack of urgency, he presumed that whoever was being tracked was unaware that he had someone on his tail.

Bolan drew back into the plentiful cover, unsheathing the TEKNA. The less sound he made, the better.

He waited only a few moments before the first footsteps were close enough for their maker to be revealed by the parting of the undergrowth: a woman, unarmed, with a rucksack on her shoulder. She was splattered with mud and looked far from happy. She was wearing shorts, and one leg showed a number of scrapes and cuts, presumably from a fall, but not deep enough to make her limp.

It wasn't Elena Anders. For a moment, Bolan wondered if he'd struck it lucky, but a second look quashed that hope. Whoever this woman was, however, one thing was certain: the Seven Stars didn't like her snooping around. She yelled in fright a fraction of a second before the tree in front of her was splintered and pulped by a heavy-duty shell. The deadened cough of the rifle told the soldier that the tracker had a clear sight of the woman, but was maybe not the best shot. Good. That gave him a chance to save her—whoever she was—and to halt her pursuer.

The woman was flat on the ground, sobbing and paralyzed with fear. The undergrowth around her kept her shielded to an extent. For the moment, her assailant likely couldn't see her.

Problem was, Bolan couldn't see him, either. Or hear him. The soldier scanned the thick covering before him, but detected no movement. He needed to get the woman out of the line of fire and draw the shooter into the open.

He slipped the TEKNA back into its sheath and pulled the HK from its holster, setting it to single shot and staring into the foliage. From the damage on the tree, he could narrow down the area the bullet had come from. More than one shot would attract undue attention from the amusement park occupants. The shooter had a

rifle, and a three-shot burst would betray another presence. Bolan needed to place this as close as he could
estimate....

The woman yelped in fear again as he loosed a shot.
It crashed through the undergrowth and took a chunk
out of a tree. There was no sound to betray the presence of the gunman, and for a moment Bolan thought
the ploy had failed. But then a shadowy figure stepped
out of cover and shot again, this time in the soldier's
direction. Bolan stood firm, knowing that he was hidden and that the rifleman was firing blindly. The shot
smashed through the branches above him, high and
wide. He stood his ground, keeping out of view while
he took a sighting. Now he knew where he was firing.

He sent another single shot into the shadows, where
his quarry had retreated. The woman remained where
she was, crying gently and muttering to herself between
sobs.

Bolan watched intently as the round disappeared into
the undergrowth. There was little indication of whether
or not it had struck home. He waited, listening for any
signs of movement. The woman was starting to crawl
across the ground. If she got to her feet she would become a target again, and that was the last thing Bolan
wanted.

Who was she? If he could get her away from here,
she might be able to share some intel on the cult.

To his right, Bolan noticed a ripple in the bushes.
The last shot had not taken his man, but had been close
enough to make him change positions. He was obviously trying to get a better view of the area where Bolan

was secreted, but this brought the gunman closer to the woman's position—too close for the soldier to risk it.

He slipped the HK back into the holster and palmed the TEKNA. Picking his way through the undergrowth, he ran parallel to the path of his intended target, who was easily traceable by the rippling trail he left in his wake. Bolan, on the other hand, was able to move silently without betraying his position. He crossed in front of his prey so that he could circle around and take him from the opposite side, where he would least expect an attack.

In position, Bolan waited for the man to blunder past him. He crashed through the undergrowth within a few yards of where Bolan stood. The shooter was young, no older than his early twenties, and appeared nervous, his eyes staring wildly and his mouth clenched in a rictus of fear. He held the rifle downward, but both hands gripped it tightly enough to make the skin whiten at the knuckles. He was hyped up, and the slightest provocation could make him fire wildly.

The soldier didn't want stray shells flying around—not with the woman so close to them.

He let the man pass, and then slipped into his wake. Bolan took two steps to catch up, then snaked one arm around the man's throat, pulling him backward, while the other arm punched up, driving the knife into the shooter's kidneys. Bolan's tight squeeze on his throat strangled any cry for help, or of pain. He twisted the knife before pulling it out and stabbing the man again, this time slipping the TEKNA under the ribs and angling up. He felt the man slump against him, and braced himself for the full deadweight. He extracted the knife and stepped away, letting the enemy fall to the dirt, his eyes staring sightlessly, blood bubbling from his mouth.

Bolan took the rifle from the dead man and slung it over his shoulder. He wiped the TEKNA on the guy's shirt and sheathed it before taking stock of his surroundings.

There was no sign that anyone else had been patrolling the swamp with the rifleman. The only sounds Bolan could pick out, other than wildlife, were the sobbing and muttering of the woman.

He needed to find out who she was and what had brought her here. But first it was imperative that they get back on the road. There was no knowing how long it would be before the dead man was missed, and Bolan intended to be a long way from here when anyone from the Seven Stars came looking.

As a soft probe, this outing had not been satisfactory. Bolan could only hope that he'd be able to get some intel from the woman to make up for this. Either way, he had to get her to safety. Bolan swiftly moved back to where she crouched in the grass. She scrambled to her feet, staring wildly as she tried to back up, turn and run. Bolan realized that she could see the rifle slung across his shoulders, and was understandably panicked. Now was not the time for words. As she slipped and slithered on the damp ground, trying to get her footing, he covered the distance in a few strides and took her by the arm. She tried to scream, and he covered her mouth. She bit into his hand. He winced at the pain but kept her mouth firmly covered.

"Shut up, come with me, or else they'll get you. The man who shot at you is dead. We will be, too, unless you listen…."

He doubted that there was anyone else in immediate range, but his choice of words had the desired effect. Her eyes blazed and then registered confusion. He felt her bite relax, and he took his hand away. She had drawn blood from the edge of his palm.

"Sorry," she said as he studied the wound.

"Time for that later," he snapped, pulling her after him as he retraced his steps toward the blacktop and his sedan. She stumbled in his wake, barely keeping on her feet, her breath coming in gasps. As they approached the pull-off where he had parked, he heard voices. He stopped and gestured for her to be quiet and stay where she was. She nodded at this, and he crept forward.

Inching as close to the edge of the undergrowth as possible, Bolan could see that a sheriff's vehicle was parked just in front of his rental. The vehicle's two occupants, a man and a woman, were speaking, and Bolan could make out the static chatter of the patrol car's radio.

The two uniforms began poking around the sedan and gazing idly up and down the road. Bolan gathered that they considered the car to be abandoned. They didn't seem to be worried about what, if anything, had happened to any passengers. Both of them were carrying the excess weight around the middle that spoke of too long sitting in patrol cars with no action, and both seemed more concerned with the fact that their parking space had been taken than with anything else.

Bolan returned to the woman and explained what was happening on the road. "We've got no one on our asses from the Seven Stars," he whispered. "Are you one of them?"

She shook her head mutely.

"Then we need to wait until the sheriff's people leave. Unless they want to impound the damn car...."

"We don't have to do that," she said, finally finding her voice. It was surprisingly deep and rich for someone with such a slender frame.

"Why not?" Bolan asked.

"I bet I know them," she said with a grin. "Better lose that, though," she added, indicating the rifle he was still carrying.

She took the lead, rising and walking out toward the turnout, beckoning for him to follow. He slipped the rifle off his shoulders, losing it under a thick fern at his feet, then followed.

The woman pushed her way noisily through the bushes, Bolan a few steps behind, causing the two law enforcement officers to whirl around.

To Bolan's surprise, rather than drawn weapons, they were met with recognition. The female officer gave Bolan an appreciative once-over.

"Hey, Martha, what brings you out here? Some cockamamie UFO bullshit? Or something a little more personal?" she added, with a wink.

"Something like that," Martha replied, blushing as she glanced at Bolan.

5

The cinder block building was pitch-black inside, and as hot as a stevedore's armpit after a twelve-hour shift. About as fragrant, too. The heat bearing down on the windowless structure was sucked in and amplified until even the packed earth under Elena's body was hot as she lay flat and tried to draw some coolness from the ground beneath her. The air was unpleasantly humid. Elena had been in the building since her audience with Ricke some time before, but she had no way of judging how long that had really been. She slept intermittently. When meals were brought to her it was always daylight, but she couldn't tell what time of day, or whether they were regular. Her stomach told her it was a long time between meals, but given the portions and the quality of the food, her hunger could be deceptive.

Her only water was in a large plastic bottle that was topped up occasionally from some tepid source. It tasted foul; whoever had cleaned out the bottle after its previous use had failed—purposely or not—to do a decent job of it.

The only thing that kept her from complete despair

was the knowledge that Ricke was no fool. Mad, yes, but not stupid. He didn't want her to die. She had information that he wanted, and in order to get it he had to keep her alive. That was something to cling to when it seemed as though the only way out of the cinder block building would be death.

If she could get out, then she might have another crack at escaping the compound.

If…

Right now, she had no strength, and her will was being sapped and drained from her like the moisture she was losing in sweat.

"Get up, bitch, the man wants you."

She blinked into the blinding brightness of the open doorway. Haloed by the light was a thin figure, a rifle dangling from his right hand.

"Duane, I—"

"I don't want to hear shit from you. You've been a big disappointment to me. The man, now, he still thinks you're worth bothering with. That's why I ain't just taken you out back and put a bullet in your head. Might do, though, if he loses patience."

His tone was conversational, which made his words all the more chilling. She had no doubt he meant what he said. Ricke could be pushed only so far. She wondered what she should offer up that would keep him interested, yet wouldn't betray any of the national secrets her father had trusted her with.

Duane stepped across the dirt floor, his silhouette blocking the light. Her eyes didn't adjust quickly enough, and so she was unprepared for the heavy kick he put into her ribs. She coughed up bile as the blow winded her, and spit it onto the floor. Before she had a chance to gather her wits, he had taken her under one armpit with his free hand and jerked her up as if she was featherlight. She scrambled to her knees and then her feet to keep up with the momentum and prevent him from dislocating her shoulder. She tripped and nearly fell as he hauled her outside.

The cinder block building—at one time a gas and oil store for the generators on some of the rides—was set away from the main residential area of the compound. Elena's muscles, cramped and aching from lack of exercise, protested as Duane strode toward the main buildings, dragging her after him. She fell and scraped her knees, ripping skin as she tried to find leverage with her feet and get upright. She squinted, finding it hard to focus in the harsh glare.

There were members of the cult nearby, going about their business. She couldn't identify them with tears filling her eyes, but she could see just about well enough to know that they were looking at her as she was dragged past. So why didn't they do anything? Were they so brainwashed that they just assumed she was a transgressor who deserved what she got? Or were they too scared to speak up or act?

Why would they? Wouldn't she have been like that herself at one point? It wasn't something that she felt comfortable admitting, but it was true....

They stopped in front of Ricke's door, and Duane banged on it. "Got the bitch," he yelled, grinning at her. "Waste of time, you ask me..."

"No one did ask you," Ricke said in an icy tone as he opened the door. He looked them both up and down with an expression of contempt and distaste. "Bring her in. I thought I told you to be careful with her," he added as he turned and walked over to his desk, seating himself behind it. He studied some papers in front of him in a staged manner, for effect, as Duane shoved Elena into a chair opposite.

"I have tried to be patient with you, my dear," Ricke continued, without glancing up. "I understand family loyalties. Truly, I do. They are the strongest emotional and psychological ties we have, and therefore the biggest obstacles to attaining our own true selves and our purest aims. That's why I'm so keen on the idea of deprogramming, to open ourselves to the truth before our eyes."

Elena wished she was back in the cinder block building. It might be a hellhole, but at least it was better than listening to the self-justifying crap Ricke was spewing.

"I was hoping you would have realized this, and realized that we can help you to help yourself. It would make your life so much easier, and that would be preferable to how it is now, would it not?" he added, in such a reasonable tone that, in her weakened state, she could almost see his point.

Almost, but not quite. "I don't know what you think I know," she began slowly, finding her mind and mouth dulled by her confinement.

"I *don't* know what you know, Elena. That is the point," Ricke interrupted. "I want you to tell me." His voice had that lilting, rhythmic quality that had sucked her in the first time she'd heard it. She tried to fight it.

"You know I worked for my father," she said with great deliberation, "and you think that made me privy to a great many things that could be of value. Monetary value, maybe. Propaganda value, for sure. Secrets and power, right? But you're forgetting one thing. My father is too good a politician, too good a statesman, to give someone with no security clearance access to any information that really mattered. I just did the copying and filing, typed a few letters for him. I can tell you things, but they're not what you want to hear."

Ricke sighed in an exaggerated fashion—again for effect—and looked up at the ceiling. "Elena, oh, really," he said softly.

Without warning, Duane stepped up and grabbed Elena's hair, jerking her head back and making her squeal. She didn't see the knife, but she could feel the cold, sharp edge at her throat.

"Lower. We don't want her dead," Ricke said calmly, flicking a finger. She felt the knife point turn and trace down her thorax until it snagged at the torn neck of her T-shirt and circled around her breast.

Ricke watched the knife's progress. "The neck is quick and final. I want neither of those. I want you to feel pain so that you'll wish it would stop. Which, of course, you can control, by telling me what I want to know."

"I...know n-nothing...." she stammered through fear and pain.

"You must know something. Something well worth knowing. Otherwise, there wouldn't be a government agent on his way here with enough weapons to take down a small army. He's out there now. Terry reported movement. Did you hear the gunshots?"

She shook her head; she hadn't been able to hear anything through those cinder block walls, and Ricke could easily be lying.

"Terry is a good boy. He knows this ground better than any agent. I think we've seen the last of that one. But he won't be the only one, I'm sure. Which means, of course, that you must know enough for them to want you back. You're a smart girl. If they keep sending men, then that means I have only a limited time to get what I want. And the methods I may be forced to use will be less than pleasant. Won't they, Duane?"

She could hear the snigger deep in Duane's chest, and felt his fetid breath on her nape.

Duane would enjoy this, given the chance....

"YOU OWE ME," Martha Ivers said with a sly smile. "I got you out of something there. Care to explain to me exactly what you were doing?"

"Apart from saving your ass? I could ask you the same question. Besides, it makes us even, the way I see it," Bolan replied as he drove back toward town. There was still very little traffic on the highway, so it wasn't difficult to see that the patrol car was following at a distance.

"I could have hidden, run, whatever. There was no saying that dude was going to nail me," she answered in a brittle voice. "Faced with two deputies, however, you had very few options."

"You forget that I saw your face," Bolan said mildly.

He paused, glancing at her long enough to note that his words had sunk in. "Another thing—if you supposedly got me out of that situation, then how come they're following to see what we do?"

She cursed under her breath, but said nothing. Since they'd been in the car, he'd gathered her name and that she was a reporter for the *Midnight Examiner*. For the benefit of the cops, he had become her photographer, and the duffel bag he carried contained camera equipment. If the deputies had asked to inspect it, he could hardly have refused without arousing suspicion. Such was the power of the tabloid over the town that the officers had taken her word at face value and deferred, which told the soldier something about the dynamics of Griffintown.

Martha had played on her acquaintance with the female deputy and talked them out of a parking violation. She had also wheedled with them to keep the matter quiet, claiming that it was something she was checking out unofficially—a sighting of a UFO in the area, the third in as many weeks—to pitch to her editor.

Bolan inferred from this that she was a junior, keen to impress, or at least that was what she wanted the deputies, and by extension, him, to think. Which rang hollow.

No matter, he'd get the truth from her in time. First, he needed to keep the law off his back. Minimum visibility was essential.

"If I take you back to your office, what kind of questions will I draw on either of us?"

"I can pass you off as a freelancer—"

"Spare me that UFO crap. That wasn't why you were there."

"It wasn't why you were there, either."

Despite himself, Bolan grinned at the belligerence in her tone. "I know you were snooping around the old amusement park. There's only one reason for that."

"The UFO story is a good one, because there have been sightings. The townspeople—"

"Maybe, but I'm not so stupid that I don't realize your paper would have covered that like a rash if there was anything to make of it. And officially, too, not just you in your spare time trying to suck up to the boss."

"You got me, smart guy. Happy?" she snapped. Bolan shrugged. "Look," she continued. "I've only been on the *Examiner* eighteen months. I was doing local shopper papers up east before that. I've got a journalism degree, but I'm not pushing for a Pulitzer. I'm a coward, okay? I just want to write crap and get paid and have a quiet life."

They were approaching the edge of town, and Bolan slowed as he entered the residential outskirts. Families were getting set for the day, going about their business. He stopped to allow a school crossing guard to usher a line of kindergarten children across.

"You know," he said, as he accelerated again, "I could believe that if not for one thing. You nearly got your head blown off back there. Now, I could call you clumsy and stupid—"

"Gee, thanks."

"I could," he continued, "but I could not say those

were the actions of a coward. You wouldn't have put yourself in that position."

"I didn't know they were going to try and shoot me," she exclaimed.

"Maybe not, but you're smart enough to know a cult like that isn't friendly. Not when they isolate themselves in that way. So you'd better level with me." They were now within sight of the *Examiner*'s parking lot.

"I *am* a coward," she said slowly, "but a curious one. My mom always said it would get me into trouble, and she was right. I've told everyone I'm looking at the UFO sightings, and it's unofficial, because my editor thinks there's nothing to them, and that I want to prove him wrong. That's bull. Well, not the part about him thinking the UFO sightings are crap. That's true, and it's good cover. The fact is I'm curious. Why do we never write about the Seven Stars? The leader, Ricke, does good business lecturing to fringe groups at universities. They recruit off the streets. They're on our doorstep and they're a ready-made source of copy, yet we've never run a single story on them. Why? I've checked our archives. As long as they've been here, not a damn word."

Bolan had pulled into the parking lot while she spoke, and watched in the rearview mirror as the patrol car glided past. He counted to ten, and it passed by again from the opposite direction.

"That's a very good question," he said. "It's not one I'm here to answer, but it has been bothering me. Just like the fact that your sheriff's office seems very keen on making sure you get to work in one piece. I suggest

I come with you into the building, just to throw them off. I don't want them following me when I leave."

"Why is that?" she asked. "I've been straight with you. How about you come clean with me?"

Bolan said nothing as he got out of the car, keeping an eye on the patrol car, which had settled by the edge of the lot. He took his duffel bag out of the backseat and went around to open Martha's door

"Don't answer, then," she muttered petulantly.

Inside, she signed him in as a guest and he was given a pass, after being eyed up by the security guard and the receptionist. He noticed that they both scrutinized the entry as he and Martha walked to the elevator.

He said nothing until they were on the editorial floor, even though he could feel her mounting resentment. He could tell it was close to boiling over as they reached her desk; he could also feel the curious stares of the few employees who were in this early. He leaned close to her and spoke quietly. "This is not a good time or place. There are things that it's better you don't know right now. Is your cell Bluetooth?"

She furrowed her brow. "Yeah—not that you're random, or anything…"

Bolan grinned and took out his phone. "I'm sending you my number. Send me yours. Tonight, keep the line free. There are things I need to do today, but maybe we should pool our intel. Just stay in the office today and away from trouble."

His tone clearly chilled her. She nodded and looked away.

Murmuring a goodbye, Bolan left her at her desk.

She was a risk, and one he hadn't bargained on. Conversely, she could have knowledge that would be invaluable.

It had been his intent to stay in the office, maybe talk with her and give the local law enforcement time to move on. But if there was any kind of connection between the amusement park and the sheriff's office, maybe it was better to be proactive....

6

Bolan headed toward the center of town. He hadn't yet had the time to get the lay of the land he would have preferred, given that the two officials who were now tailing him probably knew how to negotiate every road and trail in the county with their eyes closed. He didn't want to pilot himself down any blind alleys, so he used the GPS that came with the rental and set it for the *Examiner* building. If he got himself lost, the GPS would automatically give him a route back toward the offices, thus keeping him out of dead ends and one-ways that would trap him or give the sheriff's people an excuse to stop and arrest him.

As he took the car down the main drag, driving as though headed back to the hotel he was sure they had already checked in with, he wondered if the officers really saw him as a problem. Perhaps they were just being small-town cautious—or bored—and his instincts were working overtime.

He drove at a steady twenty-five, paying extra attention to stop signs. In his rearview, he could see that the patrol car was keeping four or five vehicles back, if possible. They were either poor at tailing or else the traffic was not as dense as they had hoped. They were appallingly obvious.

Unless that was their plan.

People ambled up and down the sidewalks on the main street, stopping to talk, and moving at a pace that was a far cry from city life. There was little chance that he could stop, get out and lose himself among them. Nonetheless, he wanted to test the man and woman in the patrol car, just stretch them a little bit, to see what would happen.

Despite the relative lack of crowds on the sidewalks, the parking spaces lining the road were all occupied. It was only by sudden acceleration and sliding in behind a convertible as it drew out that he was able to snag a spot, incurring the angry horn blast and curses of a flatbed driver who had been patiently waiting for the space.

Bolan smiled to himself and ignored the trucker as he got out of the Ford. The vehicles between his sedan and the patrol car had slid past, and as the officers drew level, the driver of the flatbed shifted his attention to them, leaning out his window and gesturing at Bolan, stating his case with profanity punctuating each sentence. As the soldier walked into the nearest store, he heard the woman deputy trying to calm the man. "Clyde, he may be an asshole, but he hasn't broken any laws."

Good, Bolan thought. That should stress them a little, make them more prone to errors of judgment.

He had walked into a drugstore, the likes of which he hadn't seen since he was a young man. He flipped through a carousel of books that, frankly, looked as if they'd been there since his youth. He thumbed through them, one eye on the outside.

The flatbed driver had been persuaded to move on, the bottleneck he was causing drawing more horn blasts from the backed-up traffic. The patrol car had double-parked, the male deputy staying behind the wheel while the woman got out and came into the store. She started to exchange small talk with the guy behind the counter.

Bolan selected two of the paperbacks and strode toward the front, dropping them beside her with a dull thump, then pulling a ten from his wallet.

"Hello again," he said mildly as the officer turned around. "Are you guys the only deputies in this town? I only ask because you're covering a lot of ground this morning. I hope your boss pays you well for it."

The deputy eyed him, seemingly unsure whether or not he was being funny. Bolan ignored this and spoke to the cashier.

"You still charging the cover price, even after all this time?" The clerk nodded, and Bolan handed over the ten. "A bargain." He turned to the deputy. "I like a quiet night in when I'm travelling. I'm not a great one for excitement."

He took his change and the books, and left her as she mumbled a few words of acknowledgment.

Back in his car, he threw the books into the backseat and fired up the engine. The patrol car was blocking him in, and Bolan slowly reversed. As he'd suspected, the cruiser didn't move as the male officer waited for his partner to rush from the store and climb in. Now the driver had no option but to reverse and give himself away, since he'd be following directly on the soldier's tail, or to find himself in front of his supposed prey.

He chose to move on, although he didn't exactly pick up speed.

Bolan grinned and set off behind the patrol car. They were now headed toward his hotel, and the GPS was giving him instructions on where to turn and head back in the direction of the *Examiner.*

He had no way of knowing if there was a direct link between the cult and the sheriff's office, but the fact that they had taken enough of an interest to follow him not just when he was with Martha, but after they had parted company, showed that the local law enforcement had suspicions about who he was and what he and Martha had been doing in the swamps so close to Eveland.

He wanted to test them further. He had little time, and the knowledge that the local law couldn't be trusted made that time so much the tighter. He followed the patrol car down the main drag as though he was still returning to the hotel. The way the driver hesitated, trying to stay ahead while keeping the Ford in his rearview mirror, was almost amusing.

When they came up to an intersection, Bolan let the cruiser car crawl across it, and then flicked his indicator and stepped on the accelerator, swerving the sedan so that it cut across the oncoming traffic onto a side street, past some small workshops and industrial units and into a residential area. He slowed fractionally to see if the patrol car was following. The angry sound of traffic back on the main drag told him that the officers had taken action that had disrupted the smooth flow.

He was reaching the end of the road, another left turn ahead of him, as recommended by the calm voice of the GPS. He slowed almost to a crawl, just enough to see the patrol car take the far corner sharply, and to make sure they saw him. He accelerated and took the turn.

Following the GPS, he took another three turns through residential areas, each time accelerating down the straightaway to get some distance, then slowing at the corner to allow the patrol car to sight him, before accelerating once more.

He was now approaching the far end of town, and was once again in sight of the looming *Examiner* building. He wondered what the deputies made of what he was doing. They hadn't turned on their sirens, which suggested that even though both parties knew what was going down, they had no desire to make it obvious.

Bolan leaned forward and reset the GPS for his hotel. The first thing the calming voice told him to do was head back onto the main drag.

That would be too easy. Besides, he was starting to enjoy this. He figured it was the closest he would come to relaxation for the next few days, so he may as well have a little fun.

He crossed the main street at the next intersection, drove past a small estate of warehousing units and into the area where the swamplands closed in on the town. Taking what was little more than a dirt road, Bolan gunned the engine and followed the GPS's instructions, adopting the same tactics as he had in the first half of the chase.

Whether or not they intended to catch him, a chase was undoubtedly what this was. Bolan was testing the sheriff's department and letting the deputies know he was aware of their intent.

The GPS led him down a number of twisting roads with much less development than the other side of Griffintown. Traffic was sparse on these streets, and as he drove, careful to keep within speed limits and give them no excuse to pull him over, he noted that the patrol car was gaining on him.

He couldn't have that. He wanted to get some distance between himself and his pursuers so that he could be waiting for them at the end of the run.

He took a left that led him back toward the main drag, then held back at the intersection, tempting them to come up close behind him as he kept an eye on the traffic signals. When the light turned yellow, he stepped on the gas and crossed the intersection, leaving the cruiser stranded as the traffic on the main street cut them off. There were more angry horns in his wake as the patrol car tried to cut through the line of cars. This was a sleepy town and the inhabitants weren't used to their sheriff's deputies breaking a sweat.

Bolan followed the GPS back to the hotel, slowing as he approached. He pulled into the parking area and stepped out of the sedan, leaning against it as he waited.

In less than two minutes, the cruiser entered the lot. Bolan said nothing, did nothing—he just watched as it passed him. The two deputies stared at him with a mix of curiosity and dislike. He had made fools of them, and they knew it. But had he made them any more of an enemy than they had already been?

No matter. Both sides were perfectly clear on where they stood. He had tested them and found them wanting, which would be useful to keep in mind in the coming hours.

The patrol car did not stop. He waited until it was out of sight before going back into the hotel.

Up in his room, he dialed Martha's number. He made arrangements to meet her in the diner on the main drag when she finished work, then brought up the intel he had from Stony Man on his tablet.

There was work to be done. After questioning the reporter, he'd have to complete that morning's interrupted recon mission.

It was going to be a long night.

WHEN BOLAN ARRIVED at the diner, Martha was already waiting for him. She was sitting at a table near the window, but he indicated that they should take a booth in the back. She followed him, trying to make small talk, but Bolan met it with silence. A waitress came over and they placed their orders. Martha waited until the waitress had walked away before she spoke again.

"You get me here and then give me the silent treatment? Is this how you treat all your dates, Mr. Matt Cooper? Do you always tell women your name after sending them your number over Bluetooth rather than actually talking to them? Tell me, are you single by any chance? Ever wonder why?"

The last comment made Bolan smile. "Yes, and yes. But then, this isn't a date."

"You do surprise me," she said archly. "So what have you got me here for, then, other than to pump me for information?"

"Call it an exchange." He shrugged.

"Somehow, not an even one, I bet," she murmured. "Why did you get me to switch seats?" she asked, changing tack.

"You're an intelligent journalist—you should be able to work it out. Tell me, have you ever had any trouble with the local law enforcement? Any harassment?"

She looked puzzled. "Why would I? Everyone around here knows what the *Examiner* is about. Let's be honest, it pays for this town."

"And that gives you immunity? Always?"

She seemed puzzled again. "Why would anyone need that?"

"Not just anyone. You," Bolan said emphatically.

She opened her mouth to speak, but he gestured for her to stop. The waitress put their food down, and Bolan waited until they were alone again before continuing. 'I had an interesting little road trip with those two deputies from earlier. I got to see quite a lot of the backside of this town while I was at it. I don't think they were very amused by it, but at least they know that I know they have their eye on me. And if those two are anything to go by, I know I can outpace and outthink them if necessary. What I'm really curious about is this— did they follow me because of me or because of you?"

"I'm not sure I understand what you're getting at," Martha said, though her tone gave her away.

Bolan chuckled. "You told me you were a coward. Maybe you think you are—"

"Oh, I am," she interjected. "No Pulitzers for me."

"But you were still sniffing around Eveland, around the Seven Stars."

"I told you. I'm wondering why we never mention them, even though they're on our doorstep. That's all."

"So how did you get out there this morning?" he asked. She gave him an innocent look that he didn't buy. "You haven't mentioned a car, and if you'd left it anywhere it would have been found by now. And if it had, you wouldn't be sitting here."

She paled. "I walked. I like walking. I set out early. Everyone knows I like to hike. What do you mean, I wouldn't be sitting here?"

Bolan could see he'd gotten under her skin. "I'll level with you as much as I can. Because I don't like innocent people getting caught in crossfire…but mostly because I'd like to know what you know, and I really don't want you getting in my way."

"I told you, I'm a coward," she said quietly.

"No, you're not," he said, in equally soft tones. "You may think you are, but you followed what your instinct told you, even though it nearly got you shot. And you'd follow it further. No, you're not a coward. You're frightened, but that's a different thing. Not a bad thing, incidentally—fear has stopped many a person from doing something stupid at the wrong moment. You just need to know when to choose your moment."

"And you do." It wasn't a question.

He assented. "There's someone inside the cult's compound that I am here to get out. I can't say who, and you really don't want to ask. All I can tell you is that this person has such importance, the cult will do anything to hold on to them. Anything. If they know you were snooping around there this morning, then you're no longer safe."

"Who are you?" she asked. He could see the fear in her eyes.

"I'm one of the good guys." He smiled. "You'll have to trust me on that. I'm going to send you a phone number. If I'm not back here in seventy-two hours, then you call that number and tell them Cooper is missing. They may already know. What they won't know until you call is whether or not they need to extract you. If I'm not out, then they do."

"The Seven Stars are a bunch of cranks—"

"That your paper never writes about? That are so wacky the sheriff's office gets interested in anyone they see snooping around there?"

She sighed. She looked frightened—too frightened to argue. Instead, she said quietly, "They paid for Eveland in cash. They ignored local bylaws in repurposing part of the park. They come into town and collect groceries once a month, and have a charge account with the general store. No one likes them, but no one says anything, either. When you mention them in the office there's silence. I haven't found out why, but the *Examiner* has shareholders who hide behind company names. Now, I know the cult has rinsed a lot of money from recruits and fund-raising. I figure that maybe they launder it through shares. Perhaps because they have a member on the board? Complaints about the Seven Stars are never dealt with by the sheriff's office. Money talks around here."

"It talks anywhere," Bolan replied. He was disappointed. Martha's information confirmed some of his suspicions, but she hadn't given him anything new or concrete to use. "The bank was raided recently."

"What would that have to do with them? Surely they wouldn't be so stupid...." She paused. "The sheriff's office hasn't exactly been proactive, though...."

"Now you're getting the idea. If they can do that this close to home, then you can see how deep it might run. This could be very dangerous for you. Please, do as I say."

She agreed, and Bolan called for the check. He wanted to get her home, see where she lived, and then call Stony Man. He needed to put a contingency in place to protect her if necessary.

Too many innocents were caught up in this already.

7

Bolan led Martha out of the diner. It was now dark, and the streets were lit in a sodium glare, the few people out either window-shopping or heading into the few bars and diners that remained open.

"You came by car?" he asked, looking up and down the street.

"On foot," she replied. "Some secret agent you are—you should have figured out by now that I go everywhere on foot."

"I'm not a secret agent," he murmured. "I wouldn't have figured you for a nondriver, that's all."

"I can drive, I just prefer to walk. It's a small town and it seems stupid to drive everywhere."

"You're being driven tonight," he said. "Just get in my car and don't ask questions."

"Are those questions along the lines of why you had us sitting at the back of the diner? Because I think I figured that one out," she said as she slid into the sedan.

"You're smart, Martha. Just don't be too smart." He got in beside her and started the car. "We were too easily seen and too easily targeted in the window seat. And right now I want to get you home safe. If the cops—or anyone else—have me to follow, then they'll leave you alone for a while."

"You're scaring me," she said bluntly as he pulled out into the traffic.

"Good," he replied. "Give me directions, and check the rearview as you do. Tell me what you see."

She looked in the mirror. A patrol car had slipped into their wake and was following at a distance. There was no traffic, but even so, the deputies made no attempt to conceal their intent.

"Now I really am scared," she whispered.

"Don't be," Bolan said softly but firmly. "I know that's easier said than done, but they have no reason to move on you if you stay home, go to the office and act normally. They'll be focused on me. Let me take their attention."

"It's not like I have a choice," she muttered bitterly, before giving him directions in a clipped, frightened tone. He drove slowly, keeping one eye on the cruiser. It stayed at the same distance the whole way, pulling onto the curb when he dropped Martha outside the white-washed clapboard house. She got out, but turned back before heading up the path. "What about you?" she asked.

"Like I told you, I have a job to do. It's best you don't know any details. Just remember what I said, and don't be afraid to do it when the time comes."

She paused, as though she was about to say something, but was unsure of the words. Bolan didn't give her the chance. He gunned the engine, pulling away from the curb with a squeal of tires.

He accelerated down the road. In the rearview mirror he could see her standing on the walk. The patrol car jerked into the road, the driver obviously caught off guard by his sudden movement. Martha watched it go past, then seemed to snap out of her indecision, and ran up the path to her house.

The soldier felt better about that—she was out of the way, and the immediate danger had been drawn off, trailing in his wake. As he negotiated the back roads of Griffintown, aiming for the highway, he slowed momentarily to allow the deputies to get him back in their sights.

The trunk of the sedan was loaded with his duffel bags. This time out, he had decided to take his full arsenal with him.

Whatever was going on inside the compound—whatever plans the cult had for Elena Anders—his need to execute this mission with alacrity had been accelerated by the journalist. The cult would have found the dead man by now. If they had links to the sheriff's office, then they would have connected the dots between Martha, himself and the corpse. Even if they hadn't made the link, Bolan had law enforcement breathing down his neck and tracking his every move. He was on a tight timeline, and it was being squeezed ever tighter.

When he reached the highway, the patrol car started to gain on him. He wondered if these deputies were the same duo who had dogged him this morning. After the way he had treated them, they would have a more personal score to settle, which might work to his advantage and make them sloppy.

Between here and the point where he intended to enter the swamplands, he needed to either lose these clowns or deal with them. The question now was how to do this and leave as little trace as possible.

The sedan rocked as a blast from a pump-action shotgun hit the back fender, forcing him to wrestle with the wheel and try to keep the speeding car on an even keel.

They were trying to blow out the tires. If they achieved that, at the speed he was traveling, there was no way he'd be able to maintain control of the vehicle. A second blast was too high, taking out the rear window and spraying fragments of glass throughout the interior. He swore loudly and ducked, managing to avoid anything more than a few nicks.

He wasn't going to give these cops the chance at a third strike. The highway was empty as far ahead as he could see, and in the rearview mirror, past the careening cruiser, there was no sign of anything, either. He had the space; it was just a matter of if he could pull it off....

Grunting with the effort of hauling the wheel on the standard transmission sedan, he pulled a hand brake turn, bumping wildly as he took the vehicle across the rumble strip between lanes. He tugged on the brake and jerked the stick shift so that the grinding gears squealed over the whine of the engine, spinning the car so that it was facing back toward town. Bolan pumped the gas and slammed the stick so hard that it jarred his wrist up to the elbow, trying to prevent the sedan from stall-

ing, and force the kind of acceleration usually reserved
for the pros.

Gunning the engine, he took the Ford past the cruiser
as it sped by on the other side of the highway. The driver
threw his car into a skid to try and turn quickly, and
as it slewed across the road, spinning, Bolan continued
on for five hundred yards before once again throwing a
hand brake turn. This time he was able to take it a little
easier, having bought himself a second or two with the
element of surprise. The patrol car had flipped over—
whether from the initial skid or from trying to compen-
sate for Bolan's second turn, he couldn't be sure. He
didn't detect any movement inside. As he sped by, Bolan
put in an anonymous call to Griffintown's emergency
dispatcher from his burner phone, reporting a single-
car crash on the highway.

As much as he'd wanted the deputies off his tail, he
hadn't meant to cause them any serious injury. It was
Bolan's policy never to lay a hand on those who de-
fended the law. Even if this county's sheriff's department was under the Seven Stars' thumb, these two were
probably just doing what they'd been told, and what
they thought they had to do to protect their community.

Once the wreckage was out of sight, Bolan slowed
down, testing the vehicle. He might still have to use the
car after he extracted Elena Anders from Eveland, and
he could ill-afford a dead engine.

The road was silent and empty as he traversed the
last few miles to the turnout he had used that morning.
The motor coughed and spluttered as he drew as far
into cover as he could. He took the duffel bags from the

back of the sedan. He had managed to pull the car into the verge of the swamplands, and took a few moments to draw more leaves and branches across it. If anyone should stop at the turnout, they would easily stumble on the vehicle, but from a distance, or even on a drive-by, this cover would serve until morning.

His original plan had been to recon in the morning, plan his ingress, attack and flight, and then execute the plan overnight. Now, he had no choice but to improvise; he had intel to work from, but would have felt happier with an on-the-ground knowledge of the park and the cult's activities. He would be carrying a passenger, and he couldn't predict what physical or mental state she'd be in. The more he could cut down the risks, the better.

Bolan took the same route he had that morning, cir-cling the swampier ground, moving close to the clearing that ran parallel to the access road, and keeping a watch for any patrols. When he reached the spot where he'd taken down the guard and rescued Martha, he noted that the body had been retrieved. There were signs of it having been dragged through the undergrowth and back toward the access road.

Unlike that morning, Bolan had left his hotel for the diner wearing a blacksuit under his loose shirt and pants, which he'd discarded in the sedan. He had also darkened his face with combat cosmetics, to better blend in with the inky shadows on his route.

He was now, he figured, running parallel to the se-curity fence around the old park. As he advanced, the foliage began to thin out, providing less cover under the glare of the gibbous moon. He would have preferred a darker night with more clouds.

On the other hand, the guard he had encountered earlier in the day had done nothing other than confirm his suspicion that the Seven Stars were not a well-trained bunch of fighters. A few criminals with some willing acolytes seemed, so far, to be the sum total. Not that he would take that for granted...

Bolan's progress had been rapid and unimpeded so far. He had expected some kind of regular guard patrol, possibly increased as a result of that morning's casualty. The complete lack of a security presence puzzled him. It made no sense, from a soldier's point of view.

Unless, of course, they had another means of defense. He now stood a couple yards from the fence, the skeletons of the deserted and derelict rides looming over him in the night sky.

So far, he hadn't used the night vision goggles, since the moon had given him enough light to go by. But as he prepared to enter the playground of the damned, he slipped the goggles over his head and secured them.

He could see the fence much more clearly. It looked unprotected, and a quick test for electrification showed that it was dead. He noticed one of the posts had recently been replaced. Very recently. He shook it and found that the concrete anchoring it to the earth had not yet set. Beyond, the jagged outlines of the buildings and rides seemed dark and lifeless. He must be a long way from where the cult congregated.

That was good. Provided the security was as lax inside the park's perimeter as it was in the surrounding swamp, he'd be able to sneak in without being disturbed. Slowly and carefully, he pushed at the pole anchoring the fence, twisting it in its moorings to loosen it. The tension of the wire fencing stopped it from crashing down.

When the post sagged sufficiently, he climbed it, letting his weight push it down to the ground on the inside of the park. He jumped off, landing softly as the wire fence sang gently in the night air and the pole sprang back up.

Bolan turned and pushed it back into place, so that to the casual observer it had never even moved.

He was in. Now to locate the target.

8

When they came for her again, Elena Anders would be ready. Her body ached all over, and she could feel the rips and tears in her muscles swelling. Dirt from the floor had ground into open scratches that would soon become sores. Her only consolation was that Duane seemed to take great delight in inflicting pain, but had no sexual desires to gratify. Unless, of course, that was the next step.

There had to be a next step, if only because she had held out so far and hadn't cracked. She had told them nothing. She'd bitten her tongue so hard that the blood had almost choked her, and the throbbing in her mouth was so painful that it distracted her from some of the other aches.

Her hands were useless right now—fuzzy gloves of pain, the nails slowly pulled from their beds by pliers, the agony almost making her pass out. Almost, but not quite. Duane knew what he was doing. When she seemed on the brink of losing consciousness he would stop, pause, wait for the waves of anguish to subside be-

fore asking her another question. Inevitably, she would
refuse to answer, and the pain would begin again.

At one point she had looked away from his sweat-
spangled face, the glittering eyes that reveled in his
task, and had seen their flickering shadows on the wall,
cast by the storm lamp that he used to light his work.
It loomed large, grotesque and almost cartoonlike—a
garish, ghastly representation of reality. Her mind was
spinning, and for a moment she'd believed she would
lose her grip on sanity.

Perversely, it was Duane who'd saved her from this
descent. In the instant when she felt things slip, he had
paused to alter his method of attack.

He had dragged her back from Ricke's rooms and
thrown her into the cinder block cell, while he went
to fetch the implements he required, and the lighting.
He had told her exactly what he intended to do to her,
before slamming the door and leaving her alone with
nothing but her own fear and imagination.

Elena was tougher than either he or Ricke had figured. Instead of pushing her down the path of falling
to pieces, the anticipation had steeled her. She was her
father's daughter when it came to determination, and
forewarned, she was able to prepare herself mentally
for the next onslaught.

Duane had started by slapping her around a little,
dragging her to her feet before putting down his tools.
He was inviting her to make a move, to try and escape.
She knew this, yet at the same time there was just that
very small chance that his overweening confidence
would let him down—a chance that was blown out of

the water with the first backhand that sent her reeling. She was weak from pain, lack of food, bad water and sleep deprivation. Even fueled by her anger and desperation, she could not muster any real venom.

Any fight she had left was driven out of her by the pile driver to her gut that knocked the breath from her and brought her to her knees. The heavily shod foot that crunched her jaw and loosened teeth was just for emphasis.

Even as she lay there suffering, she swore that she would get revenge on him somehow, some day. If she had wanted to die as an alternative to this before, all he had done was fire up the hatred that reversed her attitude. She would take all he had to give, and store it up for later.

Panting with his own exertions and excitement, Duane had finally left her, spitting in disgust on the ground by her prone body. He'd promised her he would be back, and that there were still things he could do to get her to answer Ricke's questions.

Some peace and love cult this had turned out to be. The inconsequential thought drifted through her head as she lay on the damp earth, and she laughed, harder and harder, until the laughter turned to sobbing, the salty tears stinging the scratches on her face.

Duane had left her feet. She had read enough about torture to know that toenails and the soles of the feet were a whole world of pain waiting for her. Added to this, she knew that once he attacked her feet she wouldn't be able to walk. That would mean any hope of escape would be lost. Despite the burning pain in her hands, she pulled herself to standing. She could still do this, but what the hell else could she do, now that her hands were, for the moment, so useless?

Despair flooded over her. The bastard might as well have finished her off there and then.

She sank back on her haunches, ignoring the pain, and started to cry again.

RICKE GESTURED TO the two women who were dressing him, and they left the room without a word. He was wearing a calf-length purple robe with an astrological design on the chest. Underneath, he wore purple track-suit bottoms, and he had purple sneakers on his feet. He waited until he heard the women leave before speaking.

"I take it from the way you're looking that you failed," he spit harshly.

"I can make her talk." Duane shrugged, trying to disguise the fear he felt. He was meaner and stronger than the older, flabbier Ricke, but there was something in the man's eyes that terrified him. He needed to please him, to get his approval.

"You haven't yet, Duane. Did you do everything you could, or are you going soft on her?" Ricke said.

Duane shook his head, half angry, half afraid. "No.... If I'd carried on she would have passed out, and then who knows how long before she came around. I took her to the brink, but had to hold back. She knows I'm coming again. She'll be scared."

Ricke sighed. "I should hope so. She's a stronger bitch than I would have liked, and we don't exactly have all the time in the world. I wonder if we should try something else to soften her up, break down her defenses before tackling her again?"

"I told you, sir, you give her more pain and she'll go black or go mad—"

Ricke smiled, although with little humor. "There are more ways to soften someone's resolve than with pain, Duane. Sometimes you just have to think a little. Are the acolytes ready?" he asked, seemingly changing tack.

"I guess so," Duane replied, momentarily confused. Then realization dawned: 'Yeah, yeah—they must be."

"Bring Elena to us. There's more than one way to skin a cat, Duane. You just have to pick the best one."

THE OLD DINER of the amusement park had been designed to cater to the rabid Evel Knieval fans who would flock to the place in droves. Except they had never come. Now, the large room was unrecognizable from its original design. The tables and chairs had been cleared, leaving a huge open floor scattered with rugs and cushions that had seen better days. Like the walls and the windows—which had been painted over—the furnishings were all varying shades of purple, turquoise and cobalt-blue, the colors of the Seven Stars. Framed pictures and laminated posters of Ricke hung along one wall, some of them accompanied by aphorisms from the great man. The focus point of this display was a red-white-and-black altar. These traditional occult colors suggested the origins of the guru's cobbled-together philosophy. On the altar stood a three-dimensional representation of the constellation of the seven sisters, from where, Ricke taught, mankind had originally come, and ultimately

aspired to return. Man's goal on earth was enlighten-
ment that would allow him to reach a state where he
could commune with God, who came from this region.

It was a ragbag of old ideas, dressed up with righteous indignation at the unfairness and corruption of
the modern world, and sugarcoated in a doctrine of love
and peace as the panacea for the world's ills.

And money. Like all gurus, Ricke was not above
earthly trappings to illustrate his divine guidance and
mental superiority. His problem was that most of the
acolytes he'd attracted thus far were poor or disenfran-
chised, or else had made show of leaving behind the
trappings of their past lives and families—much as
Elena had originally intended—in order to demonstrate
their worthiness. Ricke hadn't made anywhere near as
much money as he would have hoped, or as others might
assume. And now he had a large and growing family of
misfits to feed and house. For all his talk of other cells
and spreading the word person to person, apart from
a few isolated groups and individuals, this amusement
park—purchased with a loan from the owner of the *Midnight Examiner*—and the bank raids were all he had to
show. Unfortunately, his so-called fund-raisers raised
his profile more than his bank balance.

The *Examiner* link was what had led him to Eveland
in the first place. Blackmail based on a past life that the
Examiner's owner would rather put down to youthful
high spirits, leaving a corpse and Ricke—then a sports
reporter for a paper owned by the man's father—as a
witness with a long memory. Ricke was able to parlay
this into his people being left alone, but he could push

for little more. The *Examiner* owned the town, including the sheriff's office. Ricke's secret ensured the cult's immunity, but he was aware that to strain it too far would cause a backlash.

Elena Anders was the answer to the prayers he offered up to his God. A senator's daughter had to be worth something, and when he became aware of the access she had to her father's work, her value spiked. She held the key to his future riches. All he needed to do was unlock her resistance.

If pain would not do this, then there were other ways.

THE DOOR TO the cinder block cell burst open, and Duane walked in, holding a lamp. Instinctively, Elena tried to shrink back from him, but she froze at the sight of someone behind him. When Duane stepped around her, she saw that it was Susan Winkler. The woman's stony face was as expressionless as ever, but her eyes were soft as she took in Elena's injuries. She leaned down over her, her toneless voice as soft and as near emotion as it ever got. She was holding a bowl with cloudy water, and had a robe draped over her arm similar to the short purple one she was wearing.

"Honey, you should have told him what he wanted," she said without preamble as she took a wad of cotton wool and, soaking it in the water, started to bathe some of Elena's cuts and scratches. "Duane didn't enjoy what he did—he was just doing what he was told," she added.

Elena nodded. She didn't believe that, and she wasn't sure Susan did, either. But right now, if it delayed further pain, she would agree with anything.

Susan finished cleaning her wounds and helped her to her feet. "Here, hon, put this on," she said, handing Elena the robe. "You're coming with us."

Hesitantly, Elena did as she was asked. It made no sense. She had worn the robes before, and knew that they were ceremonial, saved for Ricke's sermons to his followers. During these celebrations the acolytes made obeisance to their distant God and came close to direct contact with a higher consciousness.

Of course. She wasn't that stupid, even when traumatized. Ricke must think she was a complete fool. Brutality had not worked, so he was going to use hallucinogenic substances to loosen her consciousness and resolve. Her mind raced. How could she go along with this and yet somehow prevent ingesting any substances that would have the effect he desired?

As the three of them walked across the compound, Susan and Duane flanking her, she reasoned that the hallucinogens must be in the food or drink that was served in the ceremonial hall. She had never consciously ingested anything else on these occasions, yet knew she had been drugged at some point. If she could avoid eating and drinking—at least large amounts—then she might be able to keep some hold on her sanity.

She was greeted by other acolytes, who joined them as they approached the entrance. They were welcoming and friendly, which seemed at odds with the way she had been treated, which some of them must have witnessed or heard about. Their mild demeanor showed her the grip Ricke had on them…the grip he wished to have on her.

The large hall still felt empty, even when all the members of the Seven Stars were in attendance, emphasizing for Elena how small the cult was. Yet it was still large enough to keep her in captivity.

The acolytes milled around, visibly impatient, muttering among themselves, until Ricke walked in with one of his wives on either side. He knelt before the altar, intoning something in what had always sounded to Elena like broken Arabic, but which was in all likelihood completely invented. Then he turned and faced the assembled throng.

"My friends, we are nearing the time when we will be taken from this place. The world is closing in on us and does not understand us. That is their loss, and for as long as they left us in peace, we could coexist with them. But soon we will have to uproot and find a new home, whether on this earthly plane or on another, astral level. We must be ready for this...."

Elena looked around at the collected acolytes. Their faces were rapt as they gazed at Ricke, even those of Duane and Susan. There had been a brief period when her own face would have registered the same expression, but now that she saw through him, she knew what Ricke really meant. He had information that someone was coming after him—maybe for her. That would account for his haste in trying to pump her for knowledge. If there was a standoff... She had heard of Waco and of Jim Jones and the strychnine in the Kool-Aid. Her blood ran cold. Then she heard his next words.

"Tonight we celebrate growing close to our fate. The old ones had many ways to touch God and converse with him. We shall share in their knowledge, and the manner in which they attained it. Ladies…"

His wives left his side and went into what had once been the kitchens. They returned with boxes, which they handed out among the crowd. She didn't want to take one, but Susan forced a box into her hand, causing her to wince in pain.

Elena opened the box. Inside was a squat, ugly yellow toad. She cursed. She had to give it to Ricke—this was going to be impossible to avoid.

Ricke, who was the only one without a toad, held up his hands. "There is only one way to get there, people. Take them out of the box…."

Beside her, Susan and Duane took the amphibians in their hands. Duane nudged Elena, indicating she should do the same. The look in his eyes told her he knew Ricke's plan. There was no way out. She reached in and grabbed the slimy animal, her stomach turning.

Ricke's eyes gleamed. It seemed to Elena that he was staring right at her.

"Lick the toad."

9

Eveland was a vast, sprawling estate that covered several acres. It was easy enough to negotiate with the night-vision goggles, but its seeming desertion was baffling. What little info Bolan had on the number of people in the Seven Stars was patchy, but it seemed the cult was nowhere near as large as Ricke liked to claim to the mostly indifferent public.

It was a fair bet that the members would be billeted close together. This area of the park certainly didn't seem occupied. The rides were dark, dank, and had an air of continued neglect. Bolan guessed that no one had been over this way for a long time—apart from whoever had repaired that fence paling, and perhaps whoever uprooted it in the first place.

Still, it was a fair bet that the broken fence, along with the death of the guard earlier in the day, would have put the cult on the defensive. Bolan had expected to meet resistance of some kind almost as soon as he'd entered Eveland.

The silence wasn't entirely inexplicable, however.

If the Seven Stars had limited resources, they would likely concentrate defenses around their living quarters.

He just had to locate them....

Bolan ran over the schematics of the park in his mind. He was southwest of the entrance, which was where the accommodation blocks and facilities for visitors had been located. It was a good bet that the cult was using these, so that was the logical place to head.

Was it the logical place to find the senator's daughter, though? She had appeared to be an unwilling participant in the bank raids.... Memories of pictures of Patty Hearst in the 1970s ran through his mind, and the expressions on the faces of both women were identical. And if Ricke was trying to pump her for information about her father's office, then it was a possibility that she would be kept apart from the others.

Bolan sighed. The only sure way to check this out would be to scour the whole of the park, which would take up valuable time. He checked his watch; the hours until dawn were few.

His best course would be to circle around and come at the park entrance from the northeast, covering the most ground in the least time. He set off, swiftly but cautiously, keeping the HK shouldered and palming the TEKNA from its sheath. Junk littered the overgrown paths and walkways that had been built between the rides, the engines and wheelhouses of which stood silent and vacant, with broken windows, and gaping holes where the doors had fallen from their hinges. Between the scaffolding and rails of the attractions, cars that had never seen passengers lay derelict and empty.

He slowed when he came to a section containing rows of boarded and shuttered concession stalls, and smaller fairground attractions that would have fleeced customers. These wood chalets were squat, shadowy threats—there was no knowing what might lurk within. None showed any sign of life.

But Bolan wasn't going to take chances. He checked each small building individually. All were padlocked, the corrosion and rust on the locks indicating that they hadn't been in use for a long time.

He moved past a row of these shacks and took a bend. Ahead of him a ride rose up sharply from the ground. A row of cars shaped like rockets and decorated in the red, white and blue stars and stripes of Knieval's unique take on the flag stood rusting at the base.

An old tarpaulin lay across the path, and as his foot landed on it, Bolan felt a strange unevenness beneath the canvas. He threw himself backward, rolling off the path and into the scant shelter afforded by the ride's toll booth. As he hit the back of the booth, he heard a whoosh of air, and a number of dark shadows flew over the path, where his head had been a few moments before. He stayed where he was, counting off the seconds until the shadows passed back the way they had come.

They repeated the arc with less and less force and speed before coming to rest, hanging in the air. Bolan got to his feet and walked across to examine them. Six wooden stakes, sharpened into points at each end and smeared with some kind of dark liquid that had soaked in over time and stained the wood... The stakes were attached to one of the struts on the ride by a wire cable. Clearly, the trigger had been concealed under the tarp.

The soldier had two concerns. The first was that this was unlikely to be the only booby trap, and being on the lookout for more would slow him down. His second concern was with the substance painted on the ends of the stakes. If they had caught him full on, there would have been no need for any other kind of offensive weapon. This secondary line of attack must be some kind of toxin, designed to catch those who might escape being impaled, but who would investigate the stakes afterward.

With a grim smile, Bolan finished examining the trap, taking care not to lay a finger on the stained tips. If the Seven Stars were using poisons, the traps could come in any number of forms. He moved on, slowed even more by the need for vigilance.

Bolan came upon a small collection of outhouses that seemed to serve as maintenance huts, and he finally got the break he was looking for. Ahead was a cinder block house with a padlock that gleamed in the moonlight—unlike any of the other locks he'd seen. The earth around the building was also scuffed and disturbed, suggesting people had been here recently.

He approached, quickening his pace. He pulled the listening apparatus from his duffel bag and applied it to the walls. Nothing. He moved around to the front and saw that the padlock hung open. He turned the knob and stepped inside, keeping close to the wall.

The interior was clear to him through the night vision goggles, and his stomach churned at what he saw.

There were stains on the ground that looked like blood. A foul stench filled the room and a filthy container of water sat in one corner. Footprints and scuffs in the dirt suggested a person had been dragged in a tight circle.

Someone had been tortured here, and it didn't take a wild guess to infer who the victim had been. But where was she now?

With strengthened resolve and urgency, Bolan left the cinder block building and resumed his search. The soft earth was indented with recent prints, and a faint trail led from the maintenance area toward the entrance to the park.

At least he was now sure where he would find Elena Anders. The downside was that she was likely to be in a heavily populated part of the park, and his escape route would be constrained by his limited knowledge of that area.

As he moved forward, he stayed in the shadows and took advantage of the cover provided by the rides and booths. He was cautious of further traps, and skirted two along the way—a spring trap similar to the one he'd triggered earlier, and one with a more insidious design meant to catch those who were seeking cover. A deep recess between two rides, where the engineers would have gained access to the motors, was inviting as a hiding spot. Too inviting. An examination revealed a covered pit three yards deep, with wooden stakes pointing upward, the tips stained dark once again.

How many more of these traps were scattered throughout the park? If he could secure Elena, then the best exit strategy would be the way he had come. At least he had a path to follow.

But before he could contemplate this, he had to locate her. As he approached the cluster of buildings that he assumed served as the Seven Stars' base, he noticed the noise and light emanating from one structure, while the others were dark.

He cursed as he drew closer. The entire cult seemed to be congregated in one building. While it was a good opportunity to take them out in one fell swoop, there was every chance that it would mean taking the target—and any other innocents involved—with them. Bolan couldn't risk that.

Inside, the building sounded like bedlam. The shapes behind the painted-over windows moved wildly, and the voices he could hear were raised in incoherent screams and shouts.

Just what the hell were they doing in there?

ELENA HAD TO LICK the toad's back. She was being closely watched, and there was no way she could fake it. She knew that the oozing secretion on the yellow skin held a hallucinogenic toxin. Licking it would leave her defenseless. Around her, some of the other cult members had already greedily run their tongues along the spines of their toads. Some were already starting to react, though this quick response was more likely autosuggestion than genuine intoxication.

Ricke had his eyes on her. Duane was at her elbow. There was nothing she could do, even though she knew she'd be lost if she ingested the toxin. If ever she needed a break, it was now.

Maybe she was owed some luck after the suffering of the last forty-eight hours. As the cult members worked themselves into a pitch of excitement, three of them jerked and danced across Ricke's sightline. At the same moment, another acolyte barged into Duane, knocking him to one side. As he spun instinctively to strike at the woman who had careered into him, he was for a second facing away from Elena. Only Susan still watched her, and she was likely unaware of the real significance of Elena taking the toxin into her system. She only furrowed her brow in confusion as Elena moved her head slightly so that her tongue touched the toad's belly rather than its back, brushing it as lightly as possible.

She knew that spitting would be pointless; the poison would already have been absorbed through the moist tissue of her tongue, and anyway, a hawk and spit would be too revealing. But at least she could ingest as little as possible, and try to ride out whatever effects it had.

Which were very few, as the men and women around her began to get the full hit of the drug. Twitching, convulsing, dancing like dervishes and talking in tongues... She suspected this behavior was partially dragged up from their subconscious, a mimicry of cults they'd seen in old TV documentaries and other media.

Ricke stood at the front of the crowd, now able to view the panorama unimpeded. His cold eyes fixed on her once more. Duane was upright again, keeping vigil by her side. Susan was gone, having joined the others in their hysterical mass hallucination. Elena had no idea what they were seeing, had no real desire to know, but she understood that she must try and fake it, and hope Ricke and Duane were convinced.

She began to imitate the others. It wasn't as hard as she would have liked; the small amount of poison she'd ingested was beginning to take effect, and it was all she could do to keep a hold on reality. The world around her began to blur at the edges, the cacophony in the room suddenly sounding distorted. She'd read about these things, but had never experienced them. Maybe some people liked these sensations, but she preferred to have control over herself, and now had to fight the waves of panic that were rising within her.

Some of the acolytes had left the cafeteria, and the rush of night air coming in through the doors they had thrust open hit her like a miasma, creeping and crawling over her skin.

She was still lucid enough to identify this possible means of escape. She moved with the throng as it started to gravitate toward the doors. She'd put some distance between herself and Duane, and looking back, saw him exchange a brief glance with Ricke, who gave a tiny nod. Duane followed quickly behind her. If she could just keep enough of a grip to conceal herself in the night, then she might have a chance.

Outside, the darkness seemed to be undulating in black waves, the rides spreading over the park as skeletons come to life, looming in and dipping down over her. Flames cast shadows and light over the immediate area as some of the acolytes set fire to the trash heap that had accumulated. It burned high and bright, and

Elena cursed as it lit the patches of dark that she had hoped to use as cover. At the same time, she was relieved, as a feeling of dread at the menacing blackness had started to rise unbidden within her.

She whirled with the other acolytes, who had clustered around the flames. She thought she would try to hide among them until she could make her escape, yet all they did was bump against her and hem her in.

She could see Duane on the edge of the crowd, standing on his toes to peer over the heads of the mass, to pick her out. Behind him, Ricke stood in the doorway, waiting.

She knew what he was waiting for, and she knew what she could expect if Duane dragged her back to the cinder block cell.

Duane caught sight of her—she could tell by the way he looked back at Ricke before turning and plunging into the throng.

She pushed through the dancing, wailing acolytes, their shouts and gyrations reverberating in her head, blurring her perception as her poisoned nervous system tried to cope with the sensory overload. She stumbled, then pulled herself upright with the forward momentum, and glanced over her shoulder. She paused, confused. Duane had stopped and was staring directly past her.

She turned and followed his gaze.

This poison was affecting her in an unexpected way. She could swear that a man in a combat suit had just stepped out from beneath the shadow of a roller coaster scaffold.

10

Bolan stood in the darkness, watching and waiting as the first of the cult members danced out of the building and into the moonlight. He watched as they built a fire of the trash heap and set it alight. He had no idea why they were doing this, or why they should wish to, but it was clear that they were on a different plane of reality than he was. He inferred this not just from the things they were doing, but also from their jerky, hesitant actions, the way they danced around each other as if only just noticing other people were there. They were barely in command of their senses and their motor functions. He couldn't say what kind of drug they had taken, only that they were extremely stoned.

Their intoxication would make them unpredictable, but they weren't as much of a threat in this state as they could have been sober. The chaos and revelry should make it easier for him to extract Elena Anders, but he also had no way of knowing what state she'd be in, or what challenges he'd face in whisking away a hallucinating girl.

The entire community seemed to pour out of the

building and congregate around the fire. The flickering light made it hard to identify faces, and each person was clothed in an identical purple robe.

Then he picked out a figure that moved through the crowd with more purpose than the rest of the acolytes. It was a woman, and she was obviously intoxicated, but perhaps not as much as the others. If she was, then she had an iron will that was driving her on. It looked very much as though Elena Anders was her father's daughter.

Bolan began to step out of the shadows, but held back when he saw the man behind her. He was advancing with the same sense of purpose, trailing in her wake. Bolan recognized his face from the bank raid CCTV footage. If he'd taken the drug, too, he showed no sign of it. He didn't appear armed, but his loose clothing could be concealing weapons.

Bolan paused to allow the situation to develop. He wanted to be as sure of the ground as possible before making his move.

He was glad that he'd waited when another man appeared in the doorway of the building. Even at this distance, it was obvious from his demeanor that he was stone cold sober. Through the diffused light of the blazing trash heap, the soldier could see the hard glint of his stare as he scoped out the scene.

Bolan guessed that Elena was taking this opportunity to try and make a break. Maybe she had before, or maybe she was under special supervision for some other reason—her political connections, perhaps. Either way, Bolan was certain she wouldn't get far with both Ricke and Duane on her ass.

It was go time. The young woman was coming toward him, and if he could deflect Duane, then he could get a head start before the stoned throng could get any kind of act together.

He stepped into the open, holding the HK downward so Elena wouldn't be threatened. She froze, stricken by what must have seemed like an apparition before her.

Duane kept on coming. Beyond him, Ricke had caught sight of the soldier, too. He scowled, then disappeared back inside the building. Bolan had no doubt that he was going for a weapon.

Time was of the essence.

ELENA STOPPED, UNABLE to believe what she saw.

As the man in the blacksuit broke into a run and came toward her, she heard cursing and felt a hand close around her upper arm.

"You ain't going nowhere," Duane whispered in her ear. She felt his fetid breath on her shoulder.

She was unable to form words, but together enough to take some kind of action. A wordless scream escaped her, and she pulled her arm away from him, flailing with her free hand as she twisted in his grasp. He tried to circle her waist with his other arm. She struggled, but his grip tightened.

She looked up to find the man in the blacksuit in front of her. His face was unreadable. Duane, still holding on to her, failed to respond as the man suddenly raised his rifle and struck past her with the stock, slamming it twice into Duane's face. She heard him yelp in pain, felt hot blood spatter on her arm, then his grasp slackened and he fell backward.

When the man in the blacksuit took hold of her, she offered no resistance and allowed herself to be dragged away from the trash fire and into the shadows of the deserted rides. She had no idea who he was or where they were headed, but it had to be better than what was behind her.

BOLAN STEPPED FORWARD and smashed the stock of the HK into Duane's face, splitting his nose and knocking him backward. Pain and shock stopped the man from taking any further action. But with Ricke guaranteed to return with a weapon at any moment, Bolan needed to move fast. He grabbed Elena. She was a little slack-jawed and surprised, but he could see in her eyes that she was desperately trying to make sense of what was going down. She didn't fight him.

The soldier turned and ran, pulling her after him. He was headed for the section of fencing he had used to get into the park. Their progress was slowed by Elena's unsteady gait, but she was making an effort to keep up.

Bolan reviewed their options. The majority of the cult members were too out of it to move with any kind of speed and precision. Duane was temporarily out of action, but he would be pissed as hell when he dragged himself to his feet, and that made him even more of a danger. The other problem was Ricke.

Bolan had a head start on them, but was slowed by Elena. It was time for a risk assessment. They had rounded several corners and put a lot of scaffolding between themselves and the enemy. He pulled Elena behind a boarded-up stall and faced her.

"Elena, can you understand me?" he said slowly and clearly.

She tried to nod, but her motions were jerky. "Toad...lick. Not as much as...others. Tried spit. Get away..."

Bolan nodded. "Good. You've done great so far, and I'm here to help you. But you've got to help me, too. Can you run?"

"Not good..."

"Climb? We have to get over the fence."

She smiled weakly and shrugged.

"It's okay, just do what you can, and I'll help you. You're one hell of a girl, Elena, and you stick to it. We need to make the best time we can. You ready?"

She nodded, though her eyes betrayed her worry that she was making a promise her body wouldn't let her keep. He let this slide, giving her arm an encouraging squeeze before leading her onto the path. He wondered if their head start would be enough.

He heard a burst of SMG fire, and figured it might not....

RICKE RUSHED through the temple and into the back room. There were some weapons there, though the majority were kept in the armory block. Despite their state, his people were well indoctrinated and would respond when he could get their attention. Ricke hadn't studied post-hypnotic suggestion and drug use during his psychology major for nothing. If you want to be a guru, then you have to know how to make your will count above all others.

Elena Anders represented serious money, and through her he could step up from the level his community was operating on at present. Like most cult leaders, Ricke was a strange mix of the venal and the evangelist. He believed in his message, but he also thought most people were just waiting to be taken for a ride. If anyone was going to take advantage, then why not someone like him? He wouldn't let success get away from him when he could almost taste it. He ripped an Uzi from the cupboard, then grabbed a second one. He checked that both had full magazines and then ran back to the temple's entrance, where he could see Duane picking himself up from the dirt, shaking his head and snorting out blood and mucous. Ricke cursed the stupidity of petty criminals.

All around Duane, the hyped-up acolytes danced and frolicked, lost in their own worlds. Ricke pointed the Uzi toward the sky and fired a short burst.

The scene before him froze into a tableau as the gunfire penetrated the revelers' altered states. Ricke didn't give them a chance to make any further movements.

"People," he yelled. "We have been violated. While we celebrate, an outsider has come in and taken one of our own. Elena is gone. She has been snatched, and we must get her back at all costs. Break open the armory and take your weapons. He is only one man, and we are many. We will track him down and kill him. She must not be harmed—she is one of us," he added hurriedly. "Now go. Find our sister and bring her back!"

Duane was headed for him, still clutching his nose. Ricke was glad to see a murderous glint in the criminal's eye. He tossed the second Uzi. Duane caught it with one hand, nodding as much to himself as to his leader.

"Duane, she's valuable," Ricke said. "Make sure we get her back in one piece. And don't let that fuck get the better of you this time, all right?"

Duane seethed at the implied criticism, but such was the hold Ricke had on him that he would feel his leader was right, and that he must atone. He nodded, then loped off in pursuit of Elena and the intruder.

Ricke sniffed the night air. The park was full of traps for the unwary. In his view, it was astounding that the man had gotten this far without falling foul of them. What were the chances he would be able to get out again unscathed?

DUANE FOLLOWED THE trail as far as he could. There were no visible signs of Elena and the man, but he knew the path they'd set off on, and when he found that the traps had been nullified along the route he traveled, he stopped to figure it out.

He had helped plan and set the traps with Ricke, so he knew where they all were, and as a result, he understood the layout of the park better than almost anyone in the compound. Standing there, he could see it all in his mind's eye. He figured the intruder would take the girl back past the cinder block building where she'd been kept. That was likely how'd he'd tracked her to the temple in the first place. If Duane was right, then the man had inadvertently taken a roundabout route, which meant that people could be sent to intercept at least one avenue of escape.

A slow, evil grin spread across Duane's face as he realized how the intruder had managed to get into the park so easily. The fence post that had been recently reset would be a weak point. That had to be it.

And he knew how to stop them.

Duane changed direction and headed off toward the armory. He took a shortcut that led him beneath the old roller coaster and through the wheelhouse of another deserted ride. He skipped with assurance over the coils of rope and cable that had been left there, skirting the traps he himself had laid. He arrived at the armory just as the SMGs and rifles were being handed out to the acolytes. They still looked drugged, but they displayed the purpose and assurance their leader had instilled in them.

Holding up a hand to stop them before they dispersed, Duane separated the acolytes into groups and barked orders. When each team had accepted their instructions and moved off, he set out again himself.

Let's see the bastard get out of this in one piece, Duane thought.

BOLAN LED ELENA along the route he had chosen. He'd heard nothing in the way of arms fire following that short burst, but the silence was anything but reassuring. There had been some other noises—vocal, incoherent. He figured the burst had come from Ricke and Duane to shock the troops, and now they were being marshaled. Based on what he'd seen around the fire,

Bolan didn't expect much from the acolytes, even if they were armed. On the other hand, he was all too aware of how psychotropic drugs were used to focus and hone the capabilities of some fighting forces. If Ricke had practiced this kind of control, they might have a problem.

Bolan and Elena were making good time, but their route wasn't direct, and the cult members would have a better knowledge of the park than he did.

A burst of SMG fire chopped across the night, sending bullets ricocheting off a nearby ride. Bolan stopped short and dived for cover behind some scaffolding, pulling Elena after him.

Ahead, cutting off his path, three figures approached. If he fired from here, he would give away Elena's position. He whispered to her to stay put, then dropped down and crawled across the dank earth, moving diagonally so he could find more cover without coming out onto the moonlit path.

He rose to one knee and waited for the figures to enter his sights. As they did, firing in random directions, he picked out one of them and tapped a three-shot burst. They were spread too far apart to take out with a spray, so he chose the nearest form first.

A cry told him he had at least injured his target. Enough to take him or her out of the game, at least. Only two bursts of fire answered his shots.

By the time the return fire rained down on Bolan's position, he was already back with Elena, taking her by the arm and leading her away from their hiding spot.

He was now heading off the path, trying to circle their assailants and return to ground he had already scouted. It was imperative that he stick to this as much as possible to keep the risk of traps to a minimum. But the need to move quickly and protect Elena from the marauding acolytes made this more complicated.

He'd estimated about twenty people around the fire. Three were accounted for. If they all worked in groups this size, seven or eight teams were still out there. Not great odds, but he'd faced much worse and come through, even with a passenger.

DUANE HEARD THE gunfire, heard the yelp of a man down, and smiled. If the intruder had been struck, then fine. If not, it meant that his men had intercepted their line of escape. If they had a casualty, so be it. Their target would now be moving through unfamiliar terrain, giving the Seven Stars the upper hand.

Duane liked the military. Not the thought of joining up, and the discipline that entailed, but rather the idea that he could go and fight, fuck some shit up. He loved movies about Vietnam, the thought of being thrown into chaos and thinking on your feet. The idea of stalking an enemy and running them to ground…that was cool. Which was why he was enjoying this so much, despite the pain in his head. No, in truth the broken nose was making it all the sweeter as he closed in on this bastard. The pain sharpened his sense of achievement as he lived out his fantasy.

Duane had positioned groups along the entire route between the main encampment, the cinder block cell and the fence post. One of his men would take the bas-

tard out, or else drive him right back to where Duane
stood waiting for him.

It was simple.

Or so he thought.

BOLAN LED ELENA under the dinosaur spine of a roller
coaster, across a boardwalk and behind a row of huts
that had once housed concessions. He gestured to her
to keep quiet, and when she nodded he could tell that
the fear and adrenaline in her system were clearing the
toxin and overriding its worst effects.

Ahead of him, he spotted another small group. They
were clustered together, whispering among themselves,
their postures uncertain. He had little doubt they'd been
given specific instructions, but each person was likely
vying for the easiest option.

Leaving Elena, he crept forward until the men were
in earshot. Their arguments, slowed and dulled by the
drugs still in their system, were what he'd expected.
More importantly, their attention was taken.

He shouldered the HK; he had no desire to alert anyone else to his position, and if he moved swiftly enough
he could take these three down before they could raise
any alarm. He slipped the TEKNA from its sheath. The
three men were too preoccupied to notice him until it
was too late.

Bolan took out the man nearest him with a punch to
the throat that made him fall to the ground, choking.
The soldier moved toward the second man, following
up his punch to the first with a stamp that crushed his
nose and cheekbone. Bolan feinted with his empty hand,

which his target moved to block, opening up the other side of his body. Bolan lunged and thrust upward, driving the TEKNA under the guy's ribs. As the man fell, the soldier turned, pulling the knife out and using his free hand to push the limp body back so that it landed on the last man.

The intention was to obstruct him, buying Bolan enough time to close the gap between them and take him out, too. It proved an unnecessary precaution, as the man had already fled, in such a panic that he dropped his gun as he sprinted blindly away.

Bolan began to follow—he didn't want the man to give away that something was going down—but instinct held him back. The acolyte ran past a hut and over a rumpled tarpaulin, stumbling as he did so. His foot caught a loop of wire and loosened a stake that scythed between two huts, its arc vicious and true. The point caught the man at neck level, slicing his head from his body, which continued forward for two steps before collapsing across the boardwalk. Meanwhile the head was propelled backward, flying past Bolan and hitting the ground with a wet thump.

Dodging this gruesome projectile was not his major problem. One man's neck had proved to be little resistance to the stake, which continued on its course. Bolan had avoided being struck, but could do nothing as the stake hit a metal strut with a resounding clang, sending splinters of thick wood flying off. Bolan winced as a chunk sliced through the material of his blacksuit and into his thigh. He cursed as he pulled it out and squeezed to remove any smaller splinters.

He looked down at the wood in his hand and cursed again. Even in the shadows he could see that one end of the long splinter was much darker than the white wood farther down. If he was lucky, the stain was his own blood. If not, then he had a real problem.

Bolan ran back to where he had left Elena, feeling a tightening in his thigh where the flesh was bruised and torn. He collected her, saying nothing, and got her running again so she wouldn't have time to take in the headless corpse.

If the acolytes' plan had been to block him off and redirect him, it had failed. He was on track to get Elena over the fence and out into the open.

The sooner the better. Bolan hoped he had taken out as much of the wood as possible, but if the dark stain had not been his blood, then he didn't have long before whatever toxin had been painted on it began to take effect.

He had no way of knowing what that effect might be.

11

Ricke returned to his own rooms as soon as he had dispatched Duane to his task. Entering, he discarded the Uzi on the bed. Ricke hated guns, considered them brute instruments that lacked the subtlety of the mind. He would rather control people through his intellect and will. Nonetheless, he was pragmatic enough to know that there was a time and place for shooting at people. Now was one of those times.

His wives were waiting for him. They knew that even though the rest of the cult's orders were to search for the intruder and the missing girl, their job was to minister to Ricke's needs. He held up his arms and allowed them to strip him of his robe so that he stood naked. One of the women had a bowl of warm water, with which she attempted to bathe him. He waved her away, irritated, and took a turquoise toweling robe from another. He studied the Uzi and thought about how incongruous and idiotic he must have looked with a purple robe and an SMG.

It was time for his contingency plans. He accepted a drink from one of his wives, allowing the warm spirits to sting his mouth and burn in his throat before he picked up the phone and dialed. It rang several times. Ricke looked at the clock on his desk. It was late—or early, depending on your view—and he was not surprised that he had to wait. He reined in his impatience and tried not to let it come through when he finally heard a sleepy voice on the other end.

"Good morning," Ricke said, keeping his tone low, even, and at its most persuasive. "I wouldn't disturb you at this hour unless it was a necessity…." He waited for a few moments while his interlocutor let out a string of profanities. "Of course, you're entitled to feel like that," Ricke continued. "Entitled…if you have no love for the empire you've built up." He paused once more as he was rudely interrupted.

He made a moue of distaste at the voice on the other end. "Again, I would say you're entitled to feel like that. After all, you've spent no little time amassing your wealth and building your empire. Next to you, my own fiefdom is small. And yes, before you say so, it is in a sense dependent on you. But let us not forget why. If I fall, then I will not go down alone. And some of us have a lot further to fall, don't we?"

There was silence now on the other end of the line. Ricke allowed himself a small smile. "I thought you might see it that way. You control this town—indeed, this county—yes? So you have the power to lock down the surrounding area, with no questions asked…." He waited for the feeble protest. "No, I'm telling you this, not inquiring. I want you to mobilize the sheriff's office and have them look out for one of my people. You can't miss her, frankly—she's wearing a purple robe. There's a man with her who has taken her against her will.... Well, let's assume that he has taken her against her will. He is extremely dangerous, and I think it would be advisable for the sheriff's deputies to shoot on sight. For their own safety, of course." He waited for the reply, then smiled coldly. "Quite. I think it might be better if this never officially happened. I'm sure you can arrange that."

Ricke heard the soft click at the other end of the phone, and realized he was sweating. This situation was getting to him more than he would care to admit. He had to make another call, and by the time he was through with it, perhaps Duane would have returned and there would be no need to follow through on plan B...perhaps.

He dialed another number. This time he did not have to wait so long for an answer. A crisp voice asked what it was that he required.

"Yates, it's me," he said, attempting but failing to keep the hesitancy from his voice. He cursed himself. This was not the time to show weakness.

"What do you need?" Yates repeated.

"What we were discussing. I have something that may be of some use, and I wish to liquidate the asset as soon as possible...."

"In what form?" the arms dealer asked, his tone neutral.

"It can be in whatever form you wish. Recorded or transcribed. Sent over a secure line, by hand, or over any other kind of secure connection...."

"You sound desperate," Yates murmured with an amused, sardonic edge that set Ricke's nerves jangling.

"Not at all," he replied, measuring his words so he could keep his tone level. "I merely wish to present the information to you in the form you can best use to make a profit."

"So you expect me to pay you first, with no idea of what the content may be? Interesting…"

"Not at all—I just want to make this a swift and easy transaction for all of us."

"I'm sure you do. I'll take audio. Hard copy. I'm sure your friend can arrange for safe transportation through the county."

"He can. I'll send it by midday and give you a time of arrival," Ricke said, hoping his apprehension wasn't audible. "The agreed sum on delivery and then a percentage, as discussed?"

"Of course," Yates replied. "Midday, is it? I assume the delay is because of the little issue I raised with you?"

"That…has been raised," Ricke said.

"Quite. I would also assume, then, that you have the full audio already? Or perhaps you're selling in advance?"

"I have what you need," Ricke answered carefully.

"I see. Well, dear boy, if you deliver, I can deposit a payment into your private account, giving you something to fall back on. You'll need it when you run. If you're not being entirely honest with me, and you're still hoping to secure the goods, then I warn you…the issue will not easily go away."

"I'm aware of that," Ricke said coldly. But not as cold as the chuckle that answered him.

"I'm sure you are. I won't hold my breath."

Ricke put the phone down, his spirits sinking. Outside, he could hear the intermittent chatter of SMG fire. He hoped Yates had not heard it over the line. It was true—Ricke was treading a very thin line as he tried to secure his escape with a commodity that was still out of reach.

Dammit, what was Duane doing out there? Why wasn't the girl back in their custody?

DUANE HAD BEEN HOLDING his ground. By his reckoning, the forces he'd spread out along the route should have succeeded in cutting off the outsider's escape, and sending him back this way. That's if he hadn't wandered off track and been killed by one of the traps. Duane hoped not. His face felt as if it was on fire, and he was looking forward to taking a slow revenge on that bastard. He was sure that the outsider would have to turn back. The girl was blasted on that toad crap, and there was no way he would risk her being caught by a trap, not when he had come so far to take her alive.

Duane the military strategist—the man who had seen every Vietnam movie in the video store—was sure his plan was working. He heard another cry of pain, and a short burst of fire. That had to mean the outsider had crossed another detachment.

He steeled himself, SMG ready. He would hit the fucker with a burst at the knees, make sure he couldn't walk. Then, when he had taken the girl away from him, he would tap into each shoulder. That was supposed to hurt like hell, and it would cripple him permanently. Hell, what did that matter? The bastard wasn't going to live that long...just long enough for Duane to exact some sweet revenge.

He grinned, happy in his fantasy and eager to put it into action. It was only when the seconds stretched out to minutes, and there was no sign of the outsider or the girl, that Duane started to feel any uncertainty.

Apprehensive now, he scuttled along the side of the path, keeping himself secure, while being able to sight the whole of the boardwalk. He came around to where he had detailed a three-man team. There was no sign of them, even when he hoarsely barked their names. Worse, he caught sight of a sharpened stake moving listlessly in the still night air.

Cursing over and over, Duane closed in and stumbled over a headless body. He didn't stop to find the head. Instead, he searched for the other two men, finding one dead and the other unconscious, barely breathing through the blood and mucous that choked his smashed nose and cheekbones.

Duane rushed out onto the path, looking toward the rear of the park. If the intruder had taken the girl past these men, then he had an open course to the breach in the fence. And once he was out of the park, getting the girl back was going to be one hell of a task.

Duane lifted the Uzi above his head and let out three bursts, yelling as he did so. It would bring his soldiers running. He would marshal them, send them after the outsider. Maybe it wouldn't be too late.

He knew Ricke would hear him, too, and the boss would realize Duane had screwed up. That was another reason he needed to put this right. He wanted to shine in the eyes of his leader. Duane needed this for himself. He could not fail.

Growing impatient, he didn't wait for any of the acolytes to catch up. Instead, he set off at a run. The girl was stoned and would slow the intruder. The fence would be another obstacle. Maybe, just maybe, Duane could catch them and put this right himself. Whoever had taken Elena would know Duane's righteous wrath soon enough....

BOLAN HAD A HOME RUN to the fence. Elena was getting stronger with every step, which was a hell of a relief. The sooner the toxin was out of her system the better, especially since he could feel his thigh stiffening with every step. He couldn't afford to carry a passenger, and he would need her help if he'd absorbed some kind of toxin himself.

The paling came within sight, and he could feel her slow up a little behind him.

"They probably fixed it...it'll be stronger than ever," she muttered hesitantly.

"That was you who brought it down before?" he asked. She nodded. "You got out?" She nodded again. He grinned. "You've got guts. We're going to need them if my leg seizes up. Now, follow me...."

He took a running leap at the fence, grabbing the top of the loose pole and letting his weight pull it down slowly, just as he had when he'd entered. Elena watched for a moment, still a little dazed, before coming forward to join him. She hauled on his good leg—a thought he appreciated—and helped him bring the post down. It loosened in its mooring, coming out of the ground. It would mark their path, but the easy escape would buy them valuable time.

As they prepared to cross the sagging wire, Bolan heard the chatter of SMG fire and yelling.

"They've worked out what's happened. We need to move," he snapped, ushering her up onto the fence. She was still a little unsteady on her feet as she clambered over, but he could see that her coordination was improving.

When she reached the other side, she paused and leaned her weight against the base of the paling, keeping it as flat as possible for him. He acknowledged her gratefully as he limped over the unsteady wire screening, the wound in his leg aching.

When they were both on the other side, Bolan stared back into the park. He couldn't detect any movement, but the cult members wouldn't be long in following. He gestured to the dense, overhanging trees that threatened to intrude on the compound.

"Get in there and keep out of sight. This won't be great, but it should give us some space...."

As she obeyed him, Bolan removed a small, wrapped container of plastic explosive from one of his duffel bags. He placed three small charges at regular intervals along the fence and set the timer for two and a half minutes. That would give him and Elena a small window to get clear, and it was doubtful that the enemy would reach the fence before the blast. To delay them would be enough; to take some of them out would be a bonus.

He pulled the night-vision goggles down so that he would be able to see the way a little better, and began to lead Elena through the undergrowth. He figured that the cult members would be closing in on the fence line, but he couldn't hear anything above the sound of their own bodies moving through the foliage.

The rustling leaves and snapping branches didn't block out the sound of the explosions. Despite Bolan's best efforts, they had not made so much ground that the force of the blast and the debris thrown up by it didn't touch them. The soldier did his best to shield Elena, but they were thrown against a tree trunk and showered with mud and clods of earth and grass.

His head cracked against the wood and he swore under his breath. He was sure he'd heard some screams mingled with the sound of the blasts, and he hoped his timing had been good enough to reduce the number of enemies behind them.

But that wouldn't matter if they couldn't make better time themselves. He pulled himself upright, but swayed unsteadily as red lights flashed across his vision. He resisted the urge to shake his head and clear it, instead closing his eyes and taking a deep breath before opening them again. Elena was looking directly at him, and he could tell from her expression that she was back to normal. That was just as well, as he was feeling shaky, and was unsure whether or not this was concussion from the blow to the head, or the beginning of some kind of drug reaction.

"You okay?" she asked him.

He wanted to answer, but found it difficult to form the words. He was confused by the way her question seemed to stretch out endlessly, and her voice sounded several octaves too deep. Her head flickered and distorted as though he was looking at her reflection in a pool…a pool into which someone had just tossed a pebble, the ripples spreading out….

What the hell was happening?

"I think we'd better get moving," he said, feeling as if his mouth was crammed full of gauze. "Before this gets worse…"

12

After talking to Yates, Ricke was certain that he needed Elena and the information she carried, both as insurance and as tender. He had faith in Duane's cunning and savagery, but as this intruder was probably some kind of black ops mercenary, he knew his lieutenant would be out of his depth. Ricke changed quickly out of his robe into combat pants and boots, with a T-shirt straining over his gut. He was not as young as he once was, and the advantages of being cult leader allowed him an indulgence that was starting to show.

At first glance, he seemed the least likely figure to lead a pursuit, but on reflection, the kind of iron will that had forged this community and bartered the position he had out of nothing was not something to be ignored. Physically, he wasn't fit; mentally, he had the determination fueled by fear that could give him an edge.

He was panting hard as he ran through the park, taking the route that had already been cleared. He rarely strayed from the inhabited section around the entrance, and in the current confusion did not trust his memory of the layout of the traps. A little caution would save more time in the long run, he realized as he thudded toward the back of the park, his Uzi pointed down but his finger still in the trigger guard.

The sound of three explosions pulled him up short. He cursed and listened in the aftermath for anything that would give him a clue as to the effects of the blasts. He could hear some screams and moans. Ricke stepped up his pace, even though he could feel his lungs burn. His community was small, and if the blast had taken out too many of them, and Elena had escaped, then he had a bigger problem than he'd feared.

As the scene of devastation came into view, his curses grew louder and his pace increased. One section of fence had been ripped completely from the earth, the palings thrown into the foliage at the edge of the swamplands, the wire netting twisted and torn, strands poking up at bizarre angles. Large clumps of earth and mud had been ripped up, leaving an assault course of potholes and oozing puddles that were quickly filling up from the water that ran just beneath the surface.

Most members of the Seven Stars had reached this spot. Ricke counted sixteen in all. Five were lying on the ground in contorted positions that suggested fatality, and a closer look revealed that some were missing body parts, which brutally confirmed this suspicion. Several people sat on the ground with dazed, vacant expressions. One man was clutching his arm, the sickening angle of which betrayed a dislocation. Two others had obvious leg breaks, one with bone poking through skin and clothing. Ricke noted that Susan Winkler was tending to some of them, and he marveled at how stony and impassive her face remained even in this chaos.

Considering how close Duane must have been to the blast area, Ricke was amazed to see the man rallying the acolytes and issuing instructions. His eyes were wide and wild, set into his scorched skin. He caught his leader's gaze and walked over to where Ricke stood.

"Bastard must have had a bomb. He had her over the fence before I got here, I'm sure of that."

"And he's taken out some of us at the same time," Ricke remarked, disdaining to comment on Duane's habit of pointing out the screamingly obvious. "How many fit men do we have to go after him?"

"We'll leave Susan to tend to the wounded. So that's eight including you. You will come with us, right?" Duane's beseeching tone was pitiful. Ricke had no desire to soil his hands with this, but at the same time he felt uneasy about Duane leading the search party, considering his last act had been to lead them into a bomb blast.

That notwithstanding, he was sure Duane was correct when he said the intruder had taken the girl out into the swamps. There would be no reason for him to plant a bomb other than to create a diversion and carve out some time for himself…time that was already ticking away.

"Of course I'll be coming with you," Ricke affirmed, feeling a lurch of nausea at his lieutenant's grateful expression. "Gather the people around. We need to divide into groups and mark out our search areas."

Duane nodded. "He won't be getting far, not before

light. My guess is he's headed toward the highway. If I was him, I'd have a car ready and waiting, maybe with back-up."

"That's a reasonable deduction," Ricke said, a patronizing edge to his voice. "He won't get far. This county is sewn up."

Duane shook his head. "Well, I wouldn't be so sure about that if I was you. I know you got friends in town who keep the sheriff sweet, but let me tell you, boss, that sheriff's department is one hell of a bunch of pussies. I figure this guy could carve through them like a knife through hot butter. I wouldn't rely on them. We need to catch him before he gets to the highway."

Ricke agreed. He would have liked to believe Duane was just talking like the petty criminal he was, but his own experience of the sheriff's office told him that his lieutenant spoke the truth. Florida had one of the highest crime rates in the USA, but in this county it was almost zero. That rate had nothing to do with a lazy, corrupt sheriff's office, and everything to do with the iron grip the *Midnight Examiner* exerted on the economy of the region.

Ricke might have a hand in that, but even he had no dominion over a mercenary on the run.

Once the remaining cult members were gathered before him, Ricke divided them in half. He would lead one group, and Duane the other. They would head in opposite directions, fanning out and moving forward so that they could cover as much ground as possible.

As quickly as possible, too. Ricke glanced at the sky and could see that dawn was not far from breaking.

Once it was light, it would be easier to spot their enemy, but it would also make it easier for him to spot them. "I want Elena back," Ricke emphasized. "She is one of us. It is vital she be returned to us, and unharmed."

Instructions issued, the Seven Stars checked their weapons and redistributed those salvaged from the dead and injured. They had the firepower to take the man down. Now all they had to do was find him.

Maybe that was going to be easier than Ricke had thought. As they made to leave, the silence of the night was broken by a sudden, random burst of SMG fire. Three taps.

Duane frowned and stared at Ricke. His voice was puzzled, and perhaps a little rattled as he said, "Who the hell is he firing at?"

Bolan had pulled himself upright, taken a sighting by the stars above, and pointed them in the right direction.

"What's the matter?" Elena asked urgently.

"Some kind of toxin…a splinter from that trap in my thigh. Maybe a hallucinogen like you were given."

"How are you feeling now?" Her tone was laced with anxiety.

"Lights everywhere," he replied. He understood her insistence. She was trying to keep him focused, to make him concentrate by having to form a coherent reply. There was a lot to this girl, and another time he'd have to wonder why she had slipped into Ricke's thrall in the first place. Not now. All he could do now was keep going.

"Which way?" she queried.

"Toward the highway." Whichever direction that was. He couldn't form the words, which worried him. At least Elena was in better shape than before...maybe in better shape than he was right now.

They began to cut through the undergrowth. His initial approach to the park has been circumspect, to avoid drawing attention to himself. But now he had no such compunction. He had no one to hide from, had only to escape. He wanted to reach the highway and his sedan before sunup, and before the cult had a chance to catch up with them.

Thick, waxy leaves with stems that oozed sap twined around exposed tree roots, and twisting vines and clods of grass and mud clung to their feet, making every step an effort. The soldier took the TEKNA from its sheath and hacked at the tangled greenery blocking their path. Elena followed in his wake. He was breathing heavily as they made progress, his ears always alive to any sounds that might indicate they were being followed.

"You want me to take over?" she asked.

Bolan turned. For a moment he felt as though he was looking right through her. When his vision cleared he saw her shiver, and he registered uncertainty in her eyes. She was alone out here with a sick man—he understood her apprehension. He doubled his resolve to get them back to civilization before the toxins overtook him.

With each step, he found it harder to keep hold of who he was and what his intentions were. The black and purple of the night-vision goggles was tinged with reds, yellows and greens that bled across his eyes, turn-

ing the stark outlines of leaves and bushes into twisting, writhing shapes.

He heard a voice through his earpiece. "Striker,
you're moving close to the enemy. Three o'clock. We
have four men in a nest. Mounted grenade-launcher
trained at our lines. You need to take them down ASAP.
They've got our boys pinned."

"Roger that, Bear," Bolan muttered. "If I know these
guys, they'll be focused ahead and think their own guys
have their ass. We'll see…."

Through the trees, and the mist rising in stinking
swirls from the swamps, he could see the enemies now
to his right. Three of them were in the foxhole, one
behind the mounted Russian machine gun, keeping it
trained on the front line. The other two leaned against
the sides of the foxhole, laughing and joking in low
voices, SMGs over their shoulders. The fourth man was
off to the side, taking a leak. Not the best time to answer a call of nature.

Keeping low, Bolan circled so that he was coming
up directly behind them….

"What are you doing?"

The soldier was thrown. That was a female voice.
What was a woman doing in the Congo? There had been
no women in the detail he had just left. He turned to
face her. She was dressed in the same uniform as the
men in the foxhole. He raised his arm, ready to strike
her down with the stock of his Uzi before she could raise
an alarm. But as he caught sight of his arm, he realized
he was also in this uniform.

Of course. They were both dressed this way so

they could move freely on their approach. She must be American, one of his people. Her accent was unmistakable. Besides, there was something about her that was familiar, though he couldn't quite place her.

He let his arm drop, then noticed she was cringing away from him. He gestured for her to stay silent, and turned back toward his target. They were acting as if their position was secure. They had heard nothing.

He moved closer, until he was almost on top of them. They had made a small clearing for themselves and he was now on the edge of it. One more step and he would be out in the open. He steeled himself and took that step, even though his vision swam and he could have sworn they disappeared before his eyes.

The man taking a leak whirled around. His jaw dropped and he let the SMG fall from his shoulder to his hand in one fluid movement.

Bolan did not hesitate. One tap stitched the man across his torso, and he dropped to the ground. Within the foxhole, the sound caused a flurry of activity. The two men who had been lounging tried to turn in the enclosed space, bringing their SMGs into position as they did. It was too tight for them both to turn and sight the soldier before he tapped another burst that ended their lives. Behind them, the solider manning the RPG tried to turn around. There was no way he could use the heavy, mounted gun on the enemy at his back, but he reached down and snatched at a smaller weapon. Bolan couldn't see what it was, but he didn't care. He had only one objective: take out the enemy before he was taken out. He tapped a third time, and saw the man flail as the rounds hit him.

The nest was eliminated. Bolan should be pleased. But in his ear he heard a voice say, "Mission fail, Striker. Repeat, mission fail. Enemy has location and direction finder. They're gonna get you…."

He blinked, and when he opened his eyes he saw nothing but foliage where there should have been a foxhole and four corpses.

He spun around. Elena was staring at him. She was saying something, but for a moment it was nothing more than meaningless syllables. Gradually, the sounds resolved themselves into words.

"…do that for? They'll know where we are now. Do we know where we are? What were you shooting at?"

Elena's eyes held undisguised fear. But she didn't look threatened. What was it, then? And why wasn't she wearing that uniform? He checked his own attire. The uniform he had been wearing was also gone, replaced by a blacksuit. He struggled to work it out, before something clicked back into place.

"Where are we?" he snapped.

"Griffintown County, Florida," she said, sounding puzzled.

"Not the Congo?"

She shook her head. "What's happening?" she asked nervously, though her expression betrayed what she had already guessed.

"It's taking effect," he said bluntly. "I'm okay part of the time, but just then…." He was at a loss for words. "Well, I don't know where I was." He gazed up at the sky. The stars were starting to fade as the dawn crept closer, making it hard to take bearings from the sky alone. "I'm not even sure where we are right now," he said softly. "Did I change direction?"

"A few times," she confirmed.

Bolan cursed. He had lost track of which way he had twisted and turned while in the grip of the hallucination. Now he was in an area of swampland that didn't look familiar. Admittedly, much of it looked the same, but he had noted some landmarks during his recon. And he could hear men in the distance, crashing through the undergrowth.

Obviously, some of the cult members had made it past the explosion and were now searching the swamp for the two of them.

If the acolytes had fanned out from the site of the explosion, then they had Eveland at their backs. Bolan realized he had a marker from which to work out their position, and more importantly, the direction in which he needed to take Elena.

"Come on," he said, grabbing her arm and heading away from the approaching sounds. "We need to get out of here, quick."

13

The two groups of cult members might as have well have been one force by the time they'd started to fan out in the undergrowth. In effect, the eight men formed a long line, if a ragged and uneven one, with Ricke at one end and Duane at the other. The only thing differentiating the teams was that half of them looked to their left for leadership, and the other half to their right. Not that Ricke could offer them much in the way of direction. He had never been a fighter in the physical sense, relying much more on his sly wits to get him somewhere. Out here, he felt out of his depth, and although he wanted to make sure Duane didn't run loco and lose them the girl—who was the only asset they had left after this night—he was happy to let his lieutenant lead the way in practical matters.

"Keep in sight of the man on either side of you. That way we don't break the line," Duane whispered as they started to move apart. This message was passed on until it reached Ricke, at the far end.

The cult leader could see the sense in this. At least, doing so, they were unlikely to mow each other down in friendly fire. On the other hand, as they thrashed and hacked their way into the darker, thicker and muddier recesses of the swamplands, it became harder and harder to see more than a few yards in either direction as the greenery closed in. Although he could see that it was near dawn, and soon would be light, it didn't seem that way in the dank shadows that enclosed them under the canopy of leaves.

It was all Ricke could do to keep an eye on the man next to him. The figure slipped in and out of his line of vision as he circled trees and got lost behind sprouting grasses and plants that seemed intent on trapping them. He could hear the man fighting his way through the terrain, and the man beyond him…but how much of the sound could he attribute to his acolytes, when they were invisible to him? How did he know these noises weren't coming from the intruder as he circled back to take them down?

Ricke's paranoia was working overtime. The man who'd taken Elena was a trained soldier, possibly— make that probably—sent by the government. It wouldn't be hard for him to outwit a bunch of amateurs, some of whom were still fogged by the hallucinogen. Ricke could have cursed himself for such a lack of foresight. If he was going to drug the girl, he should have just had Duane do it in the cinder block hut. That would have been safer. Yet he'd been certain that the psychological effect of doing it as part of a ceremony would lower her resistance further, make interrogation easier.

That had been a bad call. It had been a worse one to come out here with his people. Time for him to face facts. In this maze of swamp, there was no way he could keep Duane under any kind of observation. If his lieutenant did go crazy, then by the time he reached him—even if he could find him—it would be too late to make any difference. Ricke would just have to try and ride whatever luck he had.

He dropped back off the shoulder of the man next in line, and began to go backward instead of forward. He kept the guy in sight for a while, wanting to see if he would be missed. But the acolyte was too concerned with trying to hack his way through the undergrowth to keep tabs on his leader. And perhaps wrapped up in his own fear of finding the intruder and being found wanting.

Ricke couldn't blame him, if that was the case. The last thing he wanted was to stumble across the bastard in the blacksuit. It would be far better—for him—if he got the hell back to the compound. Girl or no girl, he needed to be ready to make a run for it.

Ricke let the man move out of sight altogether, then hurried back the way he had come, stumbling as he tried to get through the foliage as fast as possible. He was panting hard, sweating so much that he felt he would slip out of his clothes. He tripped once and fell flat, hauling himself up and tumbling forward without even feeling the pain from the cuts and scratches he'd received as he went down.

By the time he was out of the thick swamps and into the defoliated area where the explosives had ripped up the earth, he was calmer. The panic had passed, and he tried to control his breathing. There was hardly anyone left in the compound—his wives and Susan Winkler, tending to the wounded—but even so, he still had his pride. He was their leader, and they must not see how rattled he was.

He stopped after he'd clambered back into the park. In answer to their questioning looks he told them that all was in hand, and that he must prepare for Duane's return with Elena. He asked solicitous questions of the wounded, and calmly left after blessing them. It was only when he was sure that he was out of sight that he started to run once more, headed for his apartments, spurred on by what he heard.

In the distance, there were exchanges of SMG fire.

BOLAN CONCENTRATED HARD. His thigh felt as if it was on fire. He needed to clean out the wound and apply a dressing and local painkiller, but there was no time for that now. Until they'd cleared the swamps, there was little he could do about the stiffness. He would have to factor this into any action he took. Normally, that wouldn't be a problem, but right now he was struggling to stay focused, and he knew that he couldn't afford to get it wrong. Not if he was going to get Elena Anders out of here.

Bolan paused to equip her with some hardware of her own.

"Have you used a gun before?" he asked, taking an Uzi from a duffel bag and handing it to her with some spare clips. "Any guns?" he added, noting the careful way she took it from him and the dubious expression on her face.

"I'd be lying if I said I was an expert, but I've used a Lee Enfield on the ranch where I grew up. And I shot some handguns for self-defense classes. I'm the only woman in Florida without a Saturday night special, though."

Bolan nodded. "So you have the basics. You can't afford to be nervous. Not now. I have no idea when this poison is going to confuse me again, and you need to be protected." He swiftly ran her through the basics of using an SMG—the way to hold it, the recoil, reloading, setting to rapid or short burst fire. Her face was rapt with concentration, and when he had finished she held the Uzi in a more assured grip, weighing it.

"I can't guarantee I'll hit anyone, but I'll make them run," she said quietly.

"That might be enough," Bolan told her, forcing a reassuring smile. He felt feverish, and the colors were leaking in his night-vision headset once again. He pulled it off. "Damn thing's no good now. Besides, it's nearly light. Can you hear anything?"

"They're out there, all right," she murmured. "Can't tell where, though…"

Bolan shook his head. His hearing was distorted by the toxin again, and he'd hoped she would be able to pinpoint the sound. "I think they've spread out," he said, "but I can't tell if they're in front or behind us."

She looked at him squarely. "It doesn't matter, does it? We have to go the right way for us, and if we run into them, then we just have to make the best of it."

"I'd rather we avoided them," Bolan replied, think-

ing of her lack of experience and his own disadvantage.
"But I guess you're right. Come on."

He beckoned for her to follow, and kept low. He'd
taken what bearings he could, but his senses were
warped by the crap running through his system. He
could feel it surging once more, the undergrowth around
them alive not with the enemy but with the rustling of
creatures the likes of which had never been seen down
in Florida. He was sure he spotted the yellow eyes of
a timber wolf staring at him, and deeper into the bush,
he made out the flashing stripes of a tiger as it slinked
between the leaves. He knew it was impossible for these
animals to be here, so he kept enough self-control to
not fire. If he saw human faces, though, he wasn't certain whether or not he'd recognize if they were real or
simply phantoms.

"Can you get a direction?" he whispered. He would
need to rely on Elena's clearer head to assist him.

She seemed to realize this, and paused to listen hard
before answering. "Shit, they're all around us. Not directly behind, but they sound like they're straight ahead
and to the left and right.... Like they're in an arc, and
we're at the center of it."

Bolan's head throbbed. The blow he'd taken earlier
had likely given him a mild concussion. That would
have been manageable under normal circumstances,
but currently it was one more thing he didn't need. The
injury clouded his thinking even more.

Just a moment too late, he could see what was happening. In their pursuit, the cult members had fanned
out in an arc, advancing so that they could trap their

prey within the circle they were forming. He guessed they intended to separate the two of them. In all likelihood, they wanted him dead and Elena alive.

He had grenades in the duffel bag, and was tempted momentarily to throw them in opposite directions. The blasts would take some of the cult members out, flush out the others.... But Bolan would also be giving away their position, and setting off explosives in this terrain could also create more problems than it would solve..

He knew what he wanted to do.

"Can you estimate distance?" he murmured.

Elena nodded. "They're not much farther than a few yards ahead, a bit more on each side. I'm surprised we can't see them," she added.

Bolan studied the thick curtain of foliage and the densely packed tree trunks. He saw ripples of movement as the less experienced cult members moved through the swamp, and if he listened hard he could make out individual footfalls into puddles of mud. Given time, he could have tracked them and silently taken them one by one, using a knife. But there wasn't time, and the stiffness and burning fire in his thigh told him it would be too difficult under present circumstances.

Two tree trunks directly to their left crossed and formed a small niche at their base. Bolan indicated for Elena to use this as shelter.

"Shoot at anything that comes near," he whispered.

"What if it's you?" she returned.

"I'll try and make sure it isn't."

She took up her position, and though she looked far from happy, there was something about the grim set of her face as she settled the Uzi into a comfortable grip that told him he wouldn't have to worry too much about her as he went about his task.

Bolan's plan was simple. Engage with the men coming directly toward him, blast through them and try to draw the straggling line away from Elena so he could pick them off. It wasn't the greatest plan he'd ever come up with. For a start, he didn't know how many men were actually out here. He figured that, with the damage he'd caused inside the park, around a dozen would cover it. Those were heavy odds, especially with the wound and toxin working against him, but they were evened up somewhat by the fact that he was a more experienced fighter.

The rustling came closer, and he stopped, settling in behind a trunk running with sticky sap. He could feel it against his cheek as he leaned forward, and concentrated on this feeling as a wave of nausea passed through him. Bolan couldn't tell if this was concussion or toxic effect, but knew above everything that he couldn't afford to have it overwhelm him now.

The wave ebbed as the greenery before him began to vibrate and shimmer with the approach of an enemy. There was a tiny clearing between his position and where the foliage grew thicker. He would wait until the man stepped into this gap before firing.

Bolan shouldered the HK and waited, with the SMG set to quick burst. He checked his surroundings again, noting the spaces he could dive into for cover. The first sound of fire would undoubtedly bring answering shots toward him.

He waited, finger tense on the trigger, until the vegetation parted and a man in a purple robe stepped through. He was wild-eyed, holding his SMG at a downward slant, and seeming more scared than anything. Part of Bolan regretted what he would have to do. This man was no soldier; he was a fool who'd found himself in a situation he didn't want to be in. But he was dangerous precisely because he was scared, and he wouldn't hesitate to shoot as soon as he saw Bolan.

Which he did. His eyes locked with the soldier's across the space of a few yards, and he jumped with fright. At the same moment his finger tightened on the trigger and he fired a burst directly into the swampy ground at his feet. The earth was torn up, mud and filthy water splattering around him.

Bolan aimed and tapped in one fluid motion, the short burst catching the man across the torso and throwing him back.

Before he even hit the grass, the soldier had moved from his position, diving into the undergrowth to his left. Bursts of answering fire chattered around him, a few stray shots taking splinters out of the tree he'd just been leaning against.

The sounds of machine gun fire were sharper and easier to pick out than the rustle of movement, and they gave him markers for where the nearest men were located. He could hear the crashing of leaves and branches as they rushed to where they thought he was, panic and inexperience overriding any caution, or instruction they may have received.

Two men emerged from the foliage. They paused,

SMGs raised, and peered across the shadowed expanse of green. That pause cost them both their lives. Bolan swiveled and fired once, taking out the man to his left at chest level. He swiveled again and took the other man with a burst that caught him as he tried to dart out of range. His head took a round as he ducked, and it burst like a ripe melon.

Bolan was already on the move. He had taken down three men, but the noise they'd created would make taking the rest that much harder. He kept low and sped toward the area where he'd left Elena. He could hear the shouts of those who were left standing, frenzied and anxious. They were trying to identify who was down, hoping their prey was one of the casualties.

That was their tough luck. They were panicking. They would make mistakes.

He would have to exploit that before the hallucinations hit him again.

14

M<small>ARTHA'S</small> <small>PHONE WENT OFF</small> at 3:00 a.m. She read the time on the old clock radio she'd kept since her days at college. It was white and clunky, and the digital panel could be kindly called retro, its green figures casting a glow across her bed. She always felt safe when she woke up and saw it standing mutely in the night, like a sentinel.

But not tonight. For some reason, she felt a churning in her gut as the phone continued to ring. She was usually a heavy sleeper, but she'd suffered a disturbed rest as the words of Matt Cooper had weighed on her. She'd barely dozed off when the phone woke her. She laid there waiting for it to cease, but it rang on and on. Giving in, she got up to answer it, despite her sense of dread.

"Martha, I hope I didn't wake you.…"

"You did," she said hesitantly. "But I guess you knew you would."

"Quite." There was forced cheerfulness in his tone, and she could hear the tension in his voice. The silence stretched out until she thought she'd have to scream.

Eventually, he spoke again. "I'm surprised you haven't asked me why I'm calling you at such an unusual hour."

She tried to make herself sound casual, but probably failed. "It must be something pretty important, Mr. Montgomery. You wouldn't call me unless it was."

David Montgomery III, owner of the *Midnight Examiner*, spent most of his time in his office, away from the newspaper staff. He seemed to be mostly concerned with living out his fantasy as a feudal lord of the area, running Griffintown County by remote control. At least that's what Martha gathered, judging by the stream of local officials who came into the building. Montgomery took only high level meetings at the paper, and the most he ever interacted with Editorial was when he called Martha's boss in to bawl him out, which seemed to be happening more and more frequently.

Maybe there was a reason for that? She had been digging at the Seven Stars for a while, and had thought her editor's dismissal of the topic was something personal. But maybe it wasn't. Maybe it was about Montgomery and what had been said behind closed doors.

As this flashed through her mind, the big boss continued. "Something's come up, Martha. Something I think only you can handle. I know you've been looking into the Seven Stars, and that your investigation has drawn only disinterest or disapproval. Well, there's been an incident that makes me think it might be the right time to focus on them. I usually dislike the idea of shitting on your own doorstep, which is why we've tended to avoid the cult. But that can't be done anymore. Your time has come, even though it is an unlikely hour," he added in a feeble attempt at lightening his tone.

Martha tried to parse his words. She thought she knew what he really meant, and she didn't like it one bit. It was time to run, and maybe call the number Cooper had given her a few hours earlier than she'd been asked.

"That's fine," she said slowly, attempting with more success than her employer to keep the tension from her voice. "I guess we all want our big break, and we just have to be ready when it comes. Give me time to get dressed, climb in the car and get my ass down to the office—"

"No, no need for that," Montgomery replied, just a little too quickly for it to be natural. "I'll send a car for you. I'll get Ramirez to send one. It'll be quicker. Just be ready in ten minutes."

Martha felt her chest tighten, fear making it hard to draw breath. Ramirez was the sheriff. Montgomery wasn't even sending his chauffeur for her, he was sending the lawmen who owed their election to his campaign fund. The lawmen she had seen at work throughout the day, tailing Cooper.

This was looking bleak.

"Okay," she replied, in as clear a voice as she could manage, hoping the fear didn't come through. "I'll be ready, boss."

"Good, good," he breathed. He almost sounded relieved.

She hung up when she heard the line click, and stood for a moment, anxiety crippling her. If she was really honest, she didn't hold out much hope for herself unless Cooper got out of Eveland alive. Even then it was a pretty slender thread.

She dressed quickly, one eye on the clock. She had seven minutes. She hoped that would be enough. She hoped whoever was on the end of the line worked nights and would answer. If not, she could kiss her ass good-bye. She hoped Montgomery's hold on the county was not so great that he could somehow block cell signals or monitor calls. If he could do the latter, she was probably a dead woman walking.

Hell, unless she did something, she was, anyway....

She took out her cell and without pausing dialed the number Cooper had sent her earlier in the evening. It rang twice.

"Martha Ivers, I presume?" said a warm, rugged voice. She was confused, but there was something about the voice that made her feel a little safer.

"Can I ask how you know who I am?"

The man chuckled. "Cooper is always very good about keeping us in the loop. I assume something has gone wrong. I wasn't expecting to hear from you until later this morning, if at all."

"You're well briefed," she replied.

"And you sound worried, Martha. So let's not waste time—tell me what's wrong. The sooner I know the sooner we can take action."

She drew a deep breath and plunged into her story. In her head, she had worked out what she needed to say, but as it came out of her mouth she realized she was babbling and had to backtrack. She had one eye on the clock and one ear on the road outside.

She finished in less than three and a half minutes. Apart from one request for clarification, the man on the other end remained silent, speaking only when she had completed her story.

"Listen carefully, Martha. We can assume from this that Cooper is in trouble, too, so we'll be arranging an extraction for both of you. Cooper can be traced from the GPS on his cell. Now that you've called me, I have the GPS for yours, so we'll be able to pinpoint where you are, and send men to recover you. In the meantime, it's best if you don't know details. You'll probably be interrogated, right?" He didn't wait for an answer. "I urge you to tell them everything you know, and spare yourself. There is nothing Cooper will have told you that can hurt him out in the field. Help is on the way. They'll know exactly where you are and will head straight for you."

Martha thanked the man and disconnected. She stood in her bedroom in a daze. Interrogation. That probably meant pain. She was such a coward.... But to tell them everything—anything—that she knew seemed so wrong, even though the man on the phone had given her the green light.

She looked at the old clock radio that had served her so well, then heard a car pull up outside. She stuffed the cell in the pocket of her jeans. They'd probably search her and take it away, right? She felt she had to take it, anyway. She couldn't think straight. All she could do was stare at the clock radio. It was ridiculous to put any kind of sentimental attachment on an inanimate object. Still, she felt incredibly sad that she probably wouldn't see the ugly piece of white plastic again. It had been a part of her life, and she felt as if that life had suddenly made an unscheduled turn. How stupid was it that, of all things, she should be focused on an old alarm clock?

Maybe it was because she didn't want to think about the people she would leave behind. Her mom, her sister...

Martha heard firm, insistent rapping on the front door. She thought for a moment about trying to run... but where? Griffintown County would be sewn up tight. The feudal lord had absolute power. She had none.

She walked to the door, opened it and was not surprised to see that Ramirez himself had answered Montgomery's command. He studied her with cold eyes, his face unreadable. Without a word, she left the house, closing the door behind her with the feeling that she was closing the door on her life.

"BEAR, THIS HAD BETTER be good. Do you know what time it is?" Brognola growled as he answered his phone. A committee meeting had kept him out until past midnight, and by the time he'd finished up at the office it had seemed like a long trek home.

"We've got a problem. Striker's contact has been taken. Chances are the big guy's in need of backup." Bear outlined all that he had been told. By the time he'd finished, Brognola was out of bed and searching for clothes.

"I'll be back at the office shortly. Meantime, anything comes in..."

"Sure. I took the liberty of authorizing a cleanup. Extraction teams for Striker and his contact. If this Montgomery guy has it as sewn up as she says—which I have no reason to doubt—then we may need more manpower. I couldn't go that far."

Despite the situation, Brognola grinned at the sardonic edge in Kurtzman's voice. "You always go too damn far. But only when you know you're right. I'll countersign, you get that backup arranged. The usual clampdown applies. It's far enough out of the way to keep it under wraps."

"Their isolation is their biggest pro and their biggest con. Consider it done." Kurtzman paused, then added, "Y'know, I'd love to find out what the connection between the Seven Stars and Montgomery is. Nothing's turned up in any background to suggest it."

"We can worry about that later," Brognola growled. "If we need to bring the hammer down on that town, we might never find out. There's work to be done."

"I hear you."

MARTHA IVERS wondered about Montgomery's connection to the Seven Stars for the entire trip to the *Midnight Examiner* building on the other end of town. Ramirez had not been alone in the car; a deputy she vaguely recognized was riding shotgun, and he'd been standing on the far side of the car as Ramirez followed her down her front walk, keeping close on her heels. The deputy, whose name she suddenly remembered—Wilkes—had watched her intently, his hand hovering near the gun on his hip. They were ready for her to run. She'd almost smiled. Where the hell could she run to?

Ramirez put her in the back of the patrol car and Wilkes slid into the front. She heard the locks click. She was secured.

The sheriff drove through the center of town, saying nothing. The deputy, too, was silent, although he occasionally glanced over his shoulder, as if to check that she was still there. A faint smile crossed his lips on one occasion, and she felt a shiver down her back. She figured that if there was any questioning to be done, then this guy would take no little pleasure in it.

At this time of the morning, Griffintown was deserted, the storefronts she knew so well staring blankly at her. Just a few hours before, the main drag had been alive. Now it was like a ghost town. She wondered how many people in the community were in thrall to Montgomery. Considering how the local economy ran, she guessed most of them were under his thumb in some way. How many knew what the owner of the *Examiner* did with that power? How many of the people she interacted with every day knew the true face of Montgomery, and were party to the darker side of his nature, as the sheriff and his staff appeared to be?

If there had been anyone on the street, would she have done something to alert them? Would it have been worth it? She felt she could trust whoever Cooper had told her to call, even though she knew nothing about him—about either man, really. But he was a friend, maybe a colleague of Cooper's. She was pretty sure something major was about to go down. That should have made her feel better, and maybe it would have if there was more time....

The only consolation she could draw was that Mont-gomery would, in all likelihood, be ground into the dust. Like Ricke and his god-awful cult. A scant consolation when it was likely too late for her.

The patrol car pulled into the parking lot. The only other vehicle on the premises was Montgomery's Ca-dillac. Ramirez and his deputy pulled Martha out of the backseat and flanked her as they led her into the build-ing. The night watchman was missing from the lobby, and Martha knew that he usually manned his post assid-uously, surfing the internet when he was supposed to be studying the CCTV. Obviously, he had been sent away.

This went deep. Too deep for her to have any hope.

They took the elevator to the third floor, saying noth-ing and avoiding eye contact. When they walked out onto the open-plan floor, it was in darkness. The only light came from the elevator and through the glass panes of the one office, in the corner.

She was used to seeing Montgomery's office in the daytime, when the paper was bustling with activity. Now, as she was led toward it, it seemed ominous.

Her imagination was working overtime. That was the journalist in her. Any other time that thought would have amused her, but right now, it just made her feel more miserable.

Montgomery watched as Ramirez and the deputy ushered her into the office. He indicated that she be seated. The two men gave her no option, a hand on each shoulder pushing her down.

She looked Montgomery squarely in the face. A puz-zled frown flickered across his features. He looked as nervous as she felt. Why should he feel like that? She remembered the tone of his voice when he had first called. But why should a man with so much money, so much power over an entire county, be nervous at all?

"You can wait outside," he told the cops, pausing until they had withdrawn. She heard the door click. She and Montgomery were, for all intents and purposes, alone.

He opened his mouth to speak, but she was quicker. "Just what are you so scared of?" she asked simply.

15

Duane cursed, loudly and repeatedly. His men looked at him as though he'd lost the plot, and maybe they were right. He was staring down at three corpses, his men, where there should have been just one—the intruder. The sky was lighter now, and he could see his surroundings clearly. Three men stood near him, and counting the three down and himself, that made seven. One was missing—Ricke.

Duane shook his head. He should have known the bastard would run when things got tough. He believed in his leader, but he wasn't so blind that he didn't realize the man was a physical coward. Why else would he have enlisted someone like Duane to do his dirty work for him?

If Ricke hadn't wanted to be part of this action, he should have said so from the start. His disappearance left Duane planning with the wrong numbers, and having to deal with the lowered morale of the remaining men. It was bad enough as it was. Duane only had to watch them gaze at the corpses and then at each other to know they were losing whatever stomach they had for the fight.

"Our leader has gone back to raise some reinforcements from his contacts. They'll be with us shortly," he lied, the words sounding hollow. He could tell the men didn't really believe him, but he felt he had to make some kind of effort. "He's good, this asshole we're tracking," Duane continued. "But these three were careless. We're not going to make that kind of mistake. We like being alive, right?"

They agreed, and Duane searched his mind frantically for some kind of plan. He scanned the immediate area, but the foliage was so thick it was impossible to see if anyone was lurking close by.

One thing, though, gave him a glimmer of hope. In the better light, he could see that the intruder had left a trail. Indentations in the mud and grass indicated that the man was dragging a leg, which meant he was injured. "We've got him," Duane breathed, pointing out the tracks. "Come on, four of us against a cripple? He's going down."

His renewed enthusiasm infected his men, whose mood seemed to brighten as they followed the intruder's path. Duane gestured for them to fan out, to make themselves harder to target with one hit. He led them from the small clearing back into the dense foliage, scenting blood and feeling his confidence grow by the second.

ELENA SAT IN THE HOLLOW formed by the tree trunks, wincing and jumping at every burst of fire. She'd realized that the man sent in after her was good, but she was horribly aware of how his injury and the poison he'd absorbed had affected him. She had no idea how many of the cult members were out here, but the law of probability suggested that one of them could easily get lucky against the weakened warrior. If that happened, where did it leave her—apart from neck-deep in shit?

The soldier had told her to stay where she was, presumably so he could come back and collect her. That was fine, but it presumed he would be alive to do that. And she had no guarantee that, in the confusing jumble of fire, his wasn't one of the screams she'd just heard. She looked up through the canopy of trees to the sky beyond. From the angle of the sun, she was able to judge which way was east. The trouble was, she had no idea where she was in relation to the road they had supposedly been headed toward. There was a car there, and a way out, even if she had to find them by herself. But which way should she go?

As frightening as it was to admit it, she was a sitting duck right now. If she stayed here, the cult would find her eventually. What would happen then was unthinkable. She would rather get lost in the swamps or die than give in to that.

Elena moved from the small hollow, stretching limbs that were starting to cramp, and being careful not to make too much noise. She glanced around, cursing the fact that the trees and shrubs were so dense. They gave her some cover, but it was impossible for her to see what lay beyond the wall of green.

She knew the general direction they'd come from, and where Eveland was in relation to their route. It meant she could work out which way they'd originally been headed. That was the way she wanted to go. That was the way to the road.

Kind of. It was all guesswork, but the harsh truth was that was all she had. Suppressing the voice that told her to stay put and wait for the soldier, she started to move toward freedom.

BOLAN ATTAINED COVER and hunkered down, breathing hard. Lights flashed before his eyes and his thigh felt as though alternating spears of ice and fire were being thrust through it. He was fighting another bout of nausea, the taste of bile filling his mouth.

He had no clear idea how many opponents were left, but he knew he wasn't in the greatest condition to face any of them. His fitness was impaired, as were his reflexes. He was slow, ill and wounded. He still had to get back to Elena, but in his current state he felt disoriented. The swamplands swirled around him. He felt his guts heave, and he leaned forward and threw up.

Spitting, he leaned back against a tree, regulating his breath. The lights were gone, and his head had cleared a little. At least this wave of side effects had hit him when he wasn't in immediate danger. With luck, he should have a little time before he felt sick again to collect Elena, and try to strike out for the highway.

He pulled himself upright and limped through grasses that tugged at his feet. He was sure he was leaving a trail, but there was little he could do about it. He had to keep moving and hope he was quicker than anyone who might get on his tail.

He'd taken note of some landmarks in the swamp after he'd left Elena, figuring he'd need them on the way back to her hiding spot. He caught sight of a crossed palm that led him onto the right trail.

He heard movement to his left, but it was retreating, so he stood silent for a moment, listening to whoever it was pass. He couldn't go on the offensive when he was so close to Elena's position. The last thing he needed was to attract attention to her. He waited until the sounds had receded into the distance, and then continued on his way.

He could see the hollow up ahead, and he quickened his pace when he saw that it was empty. Elena was gone.

Why the hell had she moved? And where had she gone? He glanced around, trying to pick up some kind of trail. She was not an experienced fighter, and despite the care she'd obviously taken, he easily picked out her path.

Bolan cursed silently. She had ventured in the direction he'd just come from. The movement he'd stopped to listen to and let pass had been, in all likelihood, the woman he'd been on his way to collect.

She was heading right into the area where he expected the remaining cult members to be gathered— where he had left three of them dead.

Bolan turned and began to hurry in her wake. He didn't take too much care about avoiding noise now. Speed was of the essence, and if it attracted the enemy to him rather than to her, then so much the better. At least she'd have a chance to run if their attack was focused on him.

DUANE MOVED HIS men slowly along the trail left by the wounded intruder, a grin of savage satisfaction curling his lips. He was going to enjoy taking out this asshole. He had wanted to do it personally, but despite the macho desire for revenge, his more cunning side told him that even with a game leg and possibly other injuries, the trained soldier would still be too much for him to take on alone. With four of them, spread out to divide his attention, there was a better chance of at least one of them being able to score a hit.

The trail was faint but visible, and the intruder had a fair start on them, even though they could move with greater ease and speed. One thing puzzled Duane. There was only the one trail, and it looked as though the man had been alone. In that case, where was Elena? Getting her back to the compound was as important as killing the intruder. Duane needed her so he and Ricke could make their escape. Both of them. Duane wasn't stupid. He knew his leader would run like hell with just the girl, given the chance. They had left one hell of a mess here already, and someone was bound to come looking for the intruder when he didn't return. Duane had no intention of being left at the compound, waiting for those reinforcements to arrive. Once he had possession of the girl, he'd have one hell of a bargaining tool.

He motioned for his men to take cover as he noticed movement in the undergrowth ahead. When they had all hidden, he shouldered his SMG and waited. Why the hell was the intruder coming back this way? It made no sense, unless...

Duane realized with a shock that the movement up

ahead was more likely to be Elena. If she emerged from
cover, he was sure that his men would fire reflexively,
before they even had time to think. If they did that, all
would be lost.

Aware that he was inviting fire on himself if he was
wrong, but terrified of taking the gamble and losing,
Duane rose and waved frantically at his men. He felt a
presence behind him and turned, slowly, to face whoever had just emerged from the curtain of green.

It was Elena.

She stood there, frozen, torn between flight and
fight. With only fifty yards between them, Duane figured it was worth trying to make a lunge for her, and he
ran a couple steps toward her before the tense silence
was broken by a wild burst of SMG fire.

Duane whirled and yelled at the man who had, in his
nervousness, let fly a burst at the girl. When he turned
back, it was too late. She had retreated, the noise and
threat breaking her hesitation. He swore and took off
after her, all caution forgotten, his men following him.

BOLAN HEARD THE burst of gunfire and broke into a run.
The direction was clear, right in line with where Elena
had been headed. There had been no scream. He hoped
this meant she hadn't been hit. If he was right, then
she'd been lucky…and so had he. There wouldn't be
a second chance, so he had to try and mop this up as
soon as possible.

He crashed through the undergrowth, fighting
against the pain in his leg. He couldn't afford to be
slowed down right now. His determination was rein-

forced by another burst of SMG fire. Then the burst turned into a chatter of exchange fire, and he felt more optimistic. It sounded as if Elena was holding her own.

CAUGHT OFF GUARD by the sight of Duane, Elena had frozen, spurred to action only by the sudden burst of bullets. Recognizing her extreme vulnerability, she had realized she needed to get back into cover before she was killed, let alone taken. She stumbled and fell, then picked herself up and ran, paying no heed to direction. That didn't matter right now. The important thing was finding some kind of cover. She knew in her gut that the only way she was going to stop them and save herself was to face them head-on.

Elena could feel every footfall jar her bones. Her injuries were throbbing and the pulse in her temple thumped painfully. She kept a tight grip on the gun Cooper had given her, despite the screaming pain in her hands and fingers. Her lungs felt as though they would burst, but she refused to give in to the burning pain in her chest. Give in, and she would be taken or killed. Not much of an option either way.

She didn't dare look back over her shoulder. If they saw where she was going, then so be it. Ahead was a small clump of bushes, about chest height, with thick, waxy leaves. It wasn't much of a hiding spot, but short of trying to clamber up a tree, and risk being a sitting target when Duane and his men caught up, it was the best she could do.

She flung herself over the top of the bush, landing on her elbow and panting. She tried to stand, and then doubled over in agony that she fought desperately. She couldn't afford to give in to this, not now. Pain was a luxury she could not afford at any cost.

She sank to her knees and raised her Uzi, sighting over the top of the bush. Her breathing and heartbeat were loud in her ears, but she could still pick out the sound of men coming toward her. In the increasing daylight, she scanned the dense, swampy forest, focusing her attention on the obvious path she'd taken. The first man through was going to get a burst. God alone knew if she would hit anyone, but she was sure as hell going to try....

Instead of one man, three burst through the foliage simultaneously, and Elena was hesitant in choosing which one to fire at first. Instead of focus, she felt panic. She fired the SMG, the recoil catching her where she had an imperfect grip. The burst went high and wide.

She hadn't hit anyone. Maybe the tops of a few trees suffered, but that was all. She swore as she tried to wrestle the Uzi back under control while ducking down behind the bush. She'd stupidly given her position away, and now she was pinned down. Plus she'd failed to score any collateral damage on her enemy.

The returning bursts of fire told her this, as if she wasn't already well aware. But none of them came directly at her. The rounds rained down on either side, intended to mark off space and trap her.

To keep her in place for as long as it took for her to use up her ammunition, get worn down and be taken alive....

16

Martha sat in the back of the patrol car, watching the dawn and knowing it would be her last. She should be thinking of her mom, her friends, the hopes and ambitions that had been thwarted on the day she'd been stupid enough to get curious about the Seven fucking Stars—as she couldn't help but think of them right now.

She would never get to write the stories she wanted, or have kids, or do anything else except end up in an anonymous hole in the ground somewhere in the swamps. She should have been thinking of that, but she wasn't. All she could think of was that if she had been a bit smarter, she could have bought herself some more time. Because she hadn't given up hope until the last few moments. As long as she'd been in the office, as long as she'd been in Griffintown…then there had been the possibility of rescue. Now that she was out here, that hope was replaced by despair. Even if the guy on the end of the phone had been playing her straight about tracking her cell, his guys would have to find her in a semitropical swamp, and by the time they fought through that.... Hell, Ramirez and his people knew this land too well to let anything slip.

She started to wonder what it would be like to die. How would they do it? Would she have to kneel in front of a hole she had dug herself, and then be shot in the back of the head? Or would they make her face the gun when it happened? Would it even be a shot, or would it be something more painful and drawn out? Wilkes had the look of a psycho about him, someone who would enjoy making it difficult. She felt as if she was going to throw up over the backseat. Her imagination—the one she'd never have the time to develop as she'd always intended—was running riot, and at exactly the wrong time.

Thinking back, she decided she had made it too easy for Montgomery. He had started to ask her questions with the air of a man who expected this to be a long and distasteful process. He had made a few threats about torture, and the propensities of the men he had working for him, before asking her about Cooper—though he hadn't known his name until she'd told him—and about her interest in the Seven Stars.

Under any other circumstances, the look on his face would have been comical. He was expecting her to claim ignorance and keep silent, whereas she'd opened her mouth and sung like a canary. Once she'd started, there had been no stopping her. She'd told Montgomery everything—how she'd become intrigued by the fact that the *Midnight Inquirer* ignored a story on its own back porch; how she had gone out to Eveland and been chased; how Cooper had saved her and how they'd been followed back to the building; what he'd told her that evening in the diner; where she thought Cooper was now and what he was doing. She shared even the most minute details, so Montgomery couldn't accuse her of leaving anything out.

But she'd also spoken at length to buy herself time. The longer she talked, the closer help was getting. If she kept it up until daybreak, the cavalry—or the military of some kind, she assumed—would ride to the rescue.

And, of course, she didn't tell him everything. The best way to hide a secret was to be open about everything else, and there was no way she was going to tell him about the number Cooper had given her, or the call she'd made. She needed to make sure she hung on to that cell for as long as possible. The fact that Ramirez and his associate had not searched her was a stroke of luck. In this case, it was a good thing that corruption had made them lazy.

When she'd finished her story, she'd sat back and asked simply, "Any questions?"

Montgomery hadn't taken that well. It was her only misjudgment during the hour or so that she'd taken to ramble through her tale. Face white with rage, he had stood up and slapped her across the face. She could still taste the blood from her split lip.

"Don't be insolent with me, you interfering bitch," he said in a cold, low tone before yelling for the sheriff and his deputy. When the two men entered, he'd barked out his orders. All the officers Ramirez had were to be sent to Eveland to hunt down Cooper and kill him. He wanted Ricke and all the cult members killed, as well. That was if the military man had left any alive in his wake.

"I want no trace of him, and I want them to look like they've gone Jim Jones on their own asses. Then burn the park. All of it. I don't want anything left."

That was when Martha had realized how deep in shit Montgomery really was. His refusal to publish anything on the cult wasn't just a matter of leaving them alone and getting on with his empire. She had always suspected that he was either tied up with the Seven Stars, or else didn't want anyone sniffing around his fiefdom, so he'd tolerated them. But from the look of cold fury—and of fear—on his face, she knew that Ricke had something on him. Why else kill them as well as Cooper? Why else raze the place?

She swore to herself that if she ever got out of this alive, then she would find out what it was. She'd do anything to nail this bastard.

Ramirez had pointed to her. "What about her?"

"Kill her," Montgomery had muttered in a perfunctory manner. "Just kill her somewhere out of the way. Do it yourself. I want to be certain."

Ramirez had nodded and grabbed her roughly by the arm, pulling her upright. She had thought for a fraction of a second about making a break for it. If she took them by surprise, she could make the elevator or the emergency stairs before they had a chance to react. She doubted they'd shoot her here; it would make too much mess that needed cleaning before morning.

But where would she run? Once she was out of the building, where could she go? She had no transport and didn't know how to hot-wire a car, and anyway, if Montgomery had the town under his thumb, a little mess on the office carpet might not even matter.

Despite the panic rising in her, she knew that her best option was to keep calm, go along with what was happening, and wait for help to come. It *would* come. It had to.

But now that she was in the patrol car and they were headed into the darker recesses of Griffintown County, she was beginning to feel she'd been giving in to blind faith. If she could somehow surprise them when they took her into the swamp, then maybe she could get away, maybe hide for long enough…? She still had the cell on her….

That was her only hope. Ramirez and Wilkes had said nothing since the sheriff started up the patrol car and gave orders to his office over the radio, sticking to the barest terms. It was a sign of how much Montgomery controlled them all that there had been no dissent—not even a query—from the dispatcher, just a monosyllabic acceptance.

As the sun rose, birds began to sing. Martha had never really been a fan of nature in the raw, and so birdsong was something that had always slipped in one ear and out the other. Today, it registered through the deputy's half-open window. The melodic, the raucous, the sweet and the dissonant. All of it was a glorious symphony, and all of it was underpinned by a low and distant hum that seemed to grow louder and more insistent.

Martha felt a surge of hope. She looked at Ramirez and Wilkes, and it seemed that they hadn't noticed the sound. Then they exchanged glances. Ramirez peered up through the windshield, trying to locate the source of the hum as it grew near. The morning was overcast, and it was only when the first of the choppers burst through the clouds that it became apparent just how close they were.

Swooping low over the highway, the copter made Ramirez curse and swerve, putting the patrol car into a skid. Martha was thrown across the backseat, her head cracking against the frame with a jarring thud.

Ignoring the throb in her skull, she stared out the back window as one chopper flew toward Griffintown and another landed about a mile down the highway. A group of armed, uniformed men dismounted and charged into the undergrowth. With a shock, she realized the patrol car had just passed the turnout where she'd emerged with Cooper almost twenty-four hours ago. She knew that if Cooper was still alive—and somehow she couldn't image anything short of a raging bull elephant taking him down—those guys would find him and whoever he'd been sent in to rescue, if he had them. As she watched, the chopper took off in the same direction as the first one, toward town.

She'd been so enthralled with what was happening down the road that she hadn't noticed what was going on here. Turning, she could see that a third chopper had circled and come down in front of them. The noise was deafening. Ramirez and his deputy seemed paralyzed, unsure of what to do.

No wonder. As the rotors started to turn slower, the hum becoming a deep, rhythmic throb, the side door of the craft slid back and six men in blacksuits jumped out, assault rifles trained on the cruiser. They were yelling something, but words were lost in the thrum of the chopper blades. Still, there was no mistaking their intent from the men's hard expressions and the gestures they made with their guns.

The detachment formed a semicircle around the police vehicle. Behind them, more men spilled out of the chopper and entered the swamplands, on the same side of the highway as their fellows had a mile down the road.

The yelling was audible now, and Martha could make out that they were ordering the sheriff and deputy to get out of the patrol car and kneel on the tarmac. The funny thing—and the relief had made her light-headed enough to actually find humor in all this—was that the two men in the front seat were so frozen in fear that they seemed ready to forfeit their lives just because they were too scared to comply.

There was a man on each side of the patrol car now, and they wrenched open the doors, pulling Ramirez and Wilkes out and throwing them flat on the highway.

Another man unlocked the rear door and opened it with a surprising gentleness that was echoed in his tone. "Martha Ivers?" He waited for her to nod before he continued. "You're safe now, ma'am. You can step out of the vehicle."

Offering her his arm, he assisted her out. As she stood up, she finally appreciated the bump on her head. She felt suddenly dizzy and stumbled against him. Then again, maybe it was a side effect of fear and relief mixed together. The man supported her and grinned encouragingly. "Steady there. It's okay, I've got you."

She gazed up at him. "You sure have. And not a moment too soon. I thought I was dead. As good as…"

"We try not to let anyone down, Martha," he said. "I think you may be in shock, which is not surprising. You've done some good work for the country tonight, I can tell you that, and I think we should get you a little medical care."

Under any other circumstances she would have complained—she didn't like being patronized, and this sounded a hell of a lot like that to her right now—but she was prepared to cut him some slack. He was only trying to help, after all, and to be frank, she didn't feel so great. She opened her mouth to tell him so, then the world closed in and went black.

THE FIRST CHOPPER landed in the parking lot of the *Midnight Inquirer* building, with two marines detailed to take the offices, while the others spread out in pairs and made their way through the streets. Despite the early hour, the sound of the approaching helicopters had woken many local residents, who had come out to watch.

The second chopper came down beside the sheriff's office, and the first three marines out secured the station in a matter of minutes. There was only the dispatcher on site, and she was on the ground, surrendering her weapon, before the group leader had a chance to finish barking the order. She was only too happy to detail Montgomery's orders, as relayed through

Ramirez, clearly hoping her cooperation would cut her some slack.

The marines locked her in one of the cells, then one took over the communications center and the others joined their fellows on the streets.

Griffintown was secured with an ease that was almost uncanny. There was no sign of any law enforcement within the town boundaries, and marines patrolling each area drew questions but no hostility from inhabitants, who tolerated Montgomery's regime out of frightened self-interest rather than loyalty.

With the town in lockdown, a detachment of marines set off in pursuit of the sheriff's men, who had headed toward Eveland. If any local lawmen encroached on the areas where the GPS revealed Cooper to be holed up, then they would wander into a killing field. But if they used the park's main entrance, they would bypass the detachments scouring the woods.

There were still a few vehicles in the sheriff's lot, which the marines piled into. Ramirez's men had a head start on them, but likely hadn't been in a real hurry. Maybe now they had some idea that they were being closed down, but up to a certain point they hadn't had any reason to rush. The marines, on the other hand, didn't hesitate to floor it.

Montgomery was sitting in his office when the two marines found him. He was leaning back in his chair, staring into space. He failed to respond when told to move away from the desk and lie flat on the floor. He failed to respond again when the order was repeated, with the caveat that punitive action would be taken if he showed any sign of hostility.

The two marines exchanged glances. Montgomery was still…too still. While one man stood to the side and covered his colleague, the second moved toward the desk. He came up close to Montgomery and looked him directly in his glassy, unblinking eyes. He reached out and touched the newspaper owner with a fingertip.

Montgomery crumpled forward over his desk, knocking over a cloudy glass of bourbon. The marine checked for a pulse and shook his head.

David Montgomery III was a realist. He knew when the game was up. He knew when he didn't want to play anymore.

17

Bolan threw himself against a tree trunk, feeling the thud all the way along his spine. He was glad of the momentary pain—it brought him back to earth, and he could not afford to start hallucinating again. He had one hell of a temperature, his thigh was burning and his head pounded. He was panting heavily, and consciously tried to control his breaths. He didn't need to add hyperventilation to his problems.

He had to focus. He was pretty certain they were down to four enemy gunmen. From the pattern of fire, he was also fairly sure they were all directly ahead of him. So was Elena. They kept firing, so he figured she was pinned down, but that they'd been unable to either score a hit or winkle her out into the open. He needed to zero in on her position and circle around. He dropped to his belly, slithering through the mud and grass. His goal was to see if he could draw their fire and also fire on them, hopefully without Elena taking him down by accident. The thought of such an irony drew a grim smile.

ELENA FELT SECURE enough in her cover, but knew she was also trapped. If she pulled back, moving away from the bushes would leave her exposed. Yet if she stayed here, she'd use up all her ammunition and leave herself a sitting target for Duane and his men. She was regretting not listening to Cooper and staying put, but it was too late for self-recrimination. She pushed those thoughts to the back of her mind and desperately scanned the area around her for anything that might give her hope.

She heard the rustling in the grasses behind her and whirled round, finger tightening on the trigger of her Uzi. She was sure the cult members had all been in front of her, and now panic gripped her. She swung the SMG in an arc, her trigger finger tensing. It was impossible to see what or who was hidden in the grass, but a swaying motion in the greenery gave its position away. She homed in on the movement....

BOLAN GLANCED UP into the barrel of an SMG. Elena had clearly heard him, and now stood facing him, wild-eyed and scared. She was about to shoot first and ask questions second. He didn't blame her, but he needed to show himself, even though he risked exposing himself to all parties.

He rose up out of the bushes for a split second, arms apart and SMG facing the sky, then hit the mud again quickly as a volley of fire sliced through the branches above him, high and wide. The bursts had come from somewhere behind Elena. Bolan crept forward, and as the grasses parted and Elena came into view again he was relieved to see that she no longer had her weapon trained on him.

"I shouldn't have moved—" she began, but he cut her short.

"You had your reasons. Right now, we need to get out of this situation. Listen…"

Hunkering into the cover of the bushes with her, he outlined his plan for getting them out of this dead end, while hopefully taking out at least some of the opposition left standing.

"I figure they're all that's left between us and the highway. Take them out of the game and we can get the hell away. Follow my lead and we'll do it." His tone carried a conviction that his raging head and throbbing leg belied, but it was enough to make her face brighten.

Leaving Elena to lay down a burst of covering fire that would attract the enemy's attention, Bolan slithered through the mud in a clockwise direction. As he'd hoped, all four men returned her fire, giving him a clear indication of their positions.

Edging into better cover, he straightened so he could move in a crouch, and at a greater speed. He could see men shifting in and out of the trees around him, but the foliage didn't move in response. They were merely shadows, which he ignored. The one thing he knew for certain was that there was a live gunman coming up on his right. Bolan watched the cult member pause in the crook of a tree to steady his aim.

The situation was in the soldier's favor. As he broke cover to advance, the gunman saw him from the corner of his eye and tried to turn and face him. Bolan would have stood little chance if not for the fact that the gunman's makeshift resting spot was his downfall.

He wrestled with his weapon to try and free it from the V in the tree. It caught on the branches, forcing him to step back and move to adjust his angle. All this took valuable time, moments in which Bolan was able to close on him, pulling the TEKNA from its sheath as he did so and shouldering his SMG. The gunman made to shout, but the cry was strangled in his throat as Bolan fell on him, pushing the cult member's weapon back and driving the knife up under his rib cage, twisting and then pulling it out.

One man down, three to go. Bolan stood up and used the crook of the tree to get his bearings on Elena's position and the other Seven Stars' hiding spots.

The second gunman was only a hundred yards away, and from where the solider was standing he could clearly see the man hunkered down and sighting the bushes where Elena was concealed. His attention had not wavered. Evidently, Bolan's assault had been as quick and clean as he'd hoped.

The time for subtlety had passed. He could feel the fever raging in his head, and knew his leg wouldn't hold out much longer. To move around and take the other three gunmen down with the TEKNA would take too long. He needed something that would eliminate one and flush the other two out of hiding and into the open, giving Elena a crack at taking one of them down.

This was what he had discussed with her. She would be ready.

Bolan still had a duffel bag with him. In it he carried the last of his grenades. He took one out and primed it, stepping back from the tree to give his arm the necessary space to arc, before throwing himself flat.

He counted off and braced for the explosion. Splinters of wood, clods of mud and grass and a shower of dirt rained around him. Before the debris even began to settle, he was up on his feet and making the ground as quickly as his nearly useless leg would allow. He could hear the remaining two gunmen yelling, abruptly breaking the eerie silence that follows any blast. They were firing wildly—he wasn't even sure if they were firing at him or just in the general direction of the explosion—and he could hear Elena's answering fire driving them back.

The area where the second gunman had been located was now not much more than a crater. That, and the fact that he could make out only two shooters up ahead, told the Executioner his plan had succeeded so far. Bolan headed for the remaining two gunmen.

The man farthest away was Duane. How he had managed to survive the blast back at the park was astounding, but the bastard obviously had nine lives, evidenced again by the way he managed to slip into the cover of the swampland while the other gunman was caught in a crossfire from Elena and Bolan. The cult member stayed upright for what seemed like an eternity as his body was cut to ribbons of blood and flesh by their bullets.

By the time he hit the dirt, Bolan was already hobbling past him, diving to take cover as Duane turned and loosed a hail of fire in his direction before finally vanishing into the undergrowth.

The soldier debated chasing him down. As long as

Duane was running free, he was a threat. But he appeared to be fleeing them, and hopefully wouldn't stop and turn back. Right now, it was a gamble Bolan was willing to take. He returned to Elena's side.

"Should we go after him?" she asked.

Bolan shook his head. "We only worry about him if he comes back our way. We need to move."

NEITHER THE GIRL nor the intruder seemed to notice that Duane had stopped running and taken position to keep them in sight. Even if he was the last of the Seven Stars left standing, Elena was his only ticket out. Judging by the way she seemed to be helping the outsider along, that asshole was about to take himself out of the game, leaving a clear path for Duane to make a move.

THE FEW REMAINING cultists had gathered at their living quarters in Eveland, the women using tarps to create makeshift stretchers for their injured comrades. They had used what medical supplies they had to try and dress wounds and splint breaks. They knew they would have to move, and one of the minivans they had garaged was brought out. They were loading the injured into the vehicle when Ricke returned. Winkler and two of Ricke's wives went straight to him, their voices a babble of questions that he silenced only by yelling over them.

"Where is everyone? Where's the girl?" Winkler reiterated, her toneless voice underlining the implicit threat in her words.

Ricke made a calming gesture. "The men are after them. Duane will sort it out and bring her back. And leave that bastard for dead, I hope," he added. "Until then, we need to continue these preparations to leave, as there will be more to follow the intruder. I'll take one of the other vehicles once Duane returns with the girl and the others. Fear not, children, I have a plan, but there is no time to explain. Just continue caring for the hurt, and be ready to follow."

Ricke left them and rushed back to his own apartment. Muttering to himself, he gathered a few clothes and a gun, throwing them into a case along with his laptop and cell. Then he uncovered the safe that he kept secreted in the room, and opened it, taking out the cash and securities he had carefully amassed for such a flight. He was counting them out and placing them in the case when Susan Winkler entered.

"What the fuck are you doing?" she asked. Even in her usual monotone, there was no mistaking the accusatory note.

Ricke turned to face her and forced a smile. "Susan, we live in a world where mammon is king, and we are forced to use their means to survive. That's why I sent you and Duane and the others to gather this money, so we could use it if a situation like this arose."

"But you're taking a separate car. And you haven't told us where we're going."

"Of course not. There hasn't been time," he said desperately. "I need to prepare, and when we're ready to depart, I'll give you the destination."

"What about Duane and the others? Doesn't sound like we're waiting for them."

"You won't be. You have the injured. For you, a head start is best. I'll take the risk and wait for them."

"Then you'll be here alone and we'll be gone. So what if you don't follow?"

Ricke feigned shock. "Susan, how could you even think such a thing? I can only believe that it's panic that has made you have such terrible thoughts. Of course I'll follow. We may even leave together, depending on how long Duane's mission takes. You must have faith, my child."

"But why should I?" she asked, moving so that she stood across the doorway.

"Because it could keep you alive at least a little while longer," Ricke said sadly. While he'd been trying to convince her, he had continued loading the suitcase. She had come in after he'd placed the gun in there, and didn't notice him reaching underneath his stack of cash as they spoke. He pulled out the small Walther that he kept for personal security.

The expression on her face was just as stony in the moment of death as it had been a second before. It seemed as though nothing affected her frozen muscles, not even the impact of a slug in her chest cavity, shattering bone and flooding her lungs with blood.

Ricke sighed as he stepped over her body, slipping the Walther into his pants pocket so he could draw it easily if there was any further dissent. Once he was outside, he noted that his wives were busy with the wounded, and seemed not to notice or care that Winkler was not with him.

"I've asked Susan to stay and wait for Duane and

the others," he began quickly. "I'll take another car.
You follow me."

Hoping that, in the heat of the moment, this had
headed off any suspicions they might have, he hurried
to get a sedan from the garage, firing it up and flinging
his suitcase in back. He pulled up alongside the minivan and got out to open the gates.

"Follow me and don't wait to close them—Susan will
see to that," he gabbled breathlessly. He was confident
he could lose the people carrier once he was out on the
highway. It was worth the risk of keeping them close
to him on the access road. If they grew suspicious and
decided to go back and check on Winkler, it would only
cause a further delay.

Ricke accelerated along the road with the minivan
on his tail. He had no idea where he would go once he
shook them off. The only thing he knew for sure was
that the government and Yates would both be on his ass,
so it was time for Ricke to retire his identity and try on
another. It was just as well that he had kept papers for
several years with his securities.

Michael Warricker had a nice, old-world ring to it.
He would enjoy being Mr. Warricker.

Ricke took a corner and slammed on the brakes as
he came up against a half-dozen sheriff's vehicles. The
sedan slewed sideways, and the people carrier crashed
into the rear fin, turning him a hundred and eighty degrees as the minivan tipped into the ditch.

Before he had a chance to recover, he was sur-
rounded by five of the sheriff's men, all armed and

aiming at him. One of the deputies hauled open the door and dragged him out.

"What the—what's going on?" he yelled.

"Sheriff's orders," returned the man who had hold of him.

Ricke turned, confused, as he heard a volley of gunfire directly behind him, and saw that some of the sheriff's men were assassinating his wives and the injured cultists in the people carrier as they lay stunned from the crash.

"Montgomery will hear about this," Ricke said, more from desperation for his own skin than from outrage at the murders.

The sheriff's man shook his head. "Way I heard it, Montgomery told Ramirez what to do. We've come to clean you up."

Ricke felt his bowels sink. So much for the new identity. It had been a decent ride, but he was screwed.

He had accepted that death was inevitable, which made the sudden hope of salvation—as unlikely as it seemed—astounding. As he stood waiting for the sheriff's man to end his life, he heard the roar of engines approaching, making all the law enforcement officers stop and turn. Before Ricke had a chance to figure out what was happening, men in blacksuits were surrounding them, yelling for the local law enforcement to drop their weapons and hit the ground. Those who were too slow, either from a desire to fight or from a stunned reaction, were drilled with one careful shot that took them out of the game. The man holding Ricke dropped his weapon and hit the dirt so fast he was almost there before his gun.

Ricke, assuming he wasn't included in the order, held out his arms and started to welcome the men. He was ecstatic in his relief.

Ecstasy was the last sensation he felt as a shot penetrated his forehead.

18

Bolan allowed Elena to support him as he hobbled through the undergrowth. They were making quicker time than he could have hoped, now. Elena was strong in spirit, and this was buoying her physical strength. She muttered encouragingly to him as she half dragged him through the swamp.

"Are we alone out here?" he interrupted at one point. She looked at him strangely. His eyes flickered around. "I can hear things, see things. It's the toxin, maybe the fever, too. I can't tell if some of them are real...."

"I can't see or hear anything," she assured him. "We're alone."

Bolan nodded, reassured, and they limped onward. He wanted to believe her, and had to take her on trust. The phantoms and shadows that flickered across his consciousness were starting to build up. When they reached the highway, he would have to ride shotgun and get her to drive. He couldn't trust himself behind a wheel.

If the soldier had been 100 percent, he would have picked up noises that Elena was not experienced enough to detect. In the distance, there were sounds of men combing the swamps, and another sound much closer…

DUANE SHADOWED THE GIRL and the intruder, waiting for his chance. He was so close, he could hear their muttered exchanges. He didn't notice the distant sounds, as he was too focused on his own objective. At first he couldn't make out why they were headed farther into the swamps and away from the highway. Then he realized how out of it the intruder was. His sense of direction was shot to shit, and Elena had no idea where they were going. Duane grinned. He'd pick off the intruder and lose the body in the mud, then drag the bitch back to the compound. Simple.

He stayed as a shadow, to their left and about ten yards behind them. The intruder was stumbling and limping badly, leaning more and more of his weight on Elena. It was only a matter of time before the asshole passed out. As soon as he did, Duane intended to step forward, take him out and knock out Elena.

Even as this plan formed, fate decided to hand him the chance on a plate. The land they were trekking through was treacherous, and as Duane watched, the intruder put his good foot into a puddle of mud that sucked his combat boot down and caused him to lurch unexpectedly. He dragged the girl off balance and she tumbled over him, landing awkwardly and cracking her shoulder against a rock. She screamed, a high-pitched yelp that told him she was hurt in a way that would make her not much of a threat. The intruder was down,

thrashing as he tried to turn on his bad thigh to get some
purchase and pull his good foot free.

He was oblivious to anything that might be happening around him. Good. Duane's grin became more vulpine as he slipped his SMG off his shoulder and stepped
from cover, crossing the yards between them in a few
long strides until he was standing over the intruder.
Duane leveled his weapon at the man's head while Elena
yelled a warning through her pain....

BOLAN TRIED TO put his weight on his bad leg to pull
himself out of the muck, but it didn't work. A searing
agony went up his thigh and into his gut. He tried to
free his foot again, both hands on his good leg, pulling
at the calf. He had to get free. Elena was hurt—he'd
heard the crack as she tumbled against the rock, and
he knew she'd broken something. He could hear noises,
see moving shapes. If any of them were real, then the
two of them were screwed. He could only hope it was
his delirium.

The sight of Duane appearing over him, grinning,
disabused him of that notion. This was no hallucination; the last man standing had returned, and he was
pointing an Uzi right at Bolan's head.

Duane sneered at him.

"Do it, then," Bolan said coldly, his voice cracked
and harsh. "Or do you only have the guts if it's an old
man, or if it's a dozen of you against two?"

Risky. He could be riling Duane to action. On the
other hand, taunting him could buy a precious second
or two.

"You ain't gonna get me that way," the cultist said in a singsong tone as snide as his expression. "I'm gonna enjoy this. And when you're ground meat, then I just take the girl and buy my ticket out of here...."

He laughed. He should have spared the soldier the lecture and just pulled the trigger. That was the difference between professionals and amateurs. Duane was no professional.

"Duane, you don't have the guts," Elena yelled, her voice trembling from tears of pain. It wasn't much, but it took his attention away from Bolan for a moment.

Bolan *was* a professional. While he'd been talking to Duane, he had pulled the TEKNA from its sheath and shifted his weight. His eyes might be clouded by pain and poison, but he had instincts and will that had been honed over years of combat. As Duane looked away for that crucial second, Bolan put everything he had into one last effort. He pulled his arm free and threw the knife at Duane's throat.

The knife missed the jugular, but caught Duane in the socket of his left eye. He screamed in pain, stumbling back and dropping the Uzi as he clawed at his face.

Bolan grabbed for his dropped SMG and tried to lever himself upright to fire....

A volley of shots rang out, jerking Duane as they caught him from behind and from the side. He fell, lifeless. Bolan had no idea what was going on, but this was sure as hell no hallucination. He could see men running toward them, and he steadied the SMG.

"Cooper...no!" yelled the man in the lead. Bo-

Ian's eyes narrowed. There was something familiar about him.

The man came over to him, dropping to his knee. As he did, he indicated two of his men to attend to Elena. There were others milling around behind them.

Bolan squinted at him. The security officer from the base in Miami?

"We've come to get you out. Not that you seemed to need too much help, there," the security man added with some good humor.

"You reckon?" Bolan asked.

"...AND YOU SHOULD see Griffintown right now. National Guard on every street corner. There's a lot of gossip, but no one really wants to say too much. The *Midnight Examiner* had such a hold on the town, and there are too many people scared of any secrets. But if no one takes over the paper, then the town will probably die. Maybe that's just as well...."

Martha finally stopped to draw breath. She and Bolan were in a visitors' lounge at the military base in Miami, where he and Elena Anders had been taken by the marine task force. Antibiotics and sterile dressings had stabilized his wounds and the effects of the toxin and infection. His leg injury was healing nicely.

"So, you planning to do some hotshot journalism?" he asked, taking advantage of her silence. "This could be worth a Pulitzer."

She laughed. "Cooper, not only am I not cut out for this kind of thing, but if I dared to write about it I'd have every security man in Florida coming through my door. It's one hell of a story, but it's not mine."

"What are you going to do?" he asked.

She shrugged. "Head back up north, maybe. Go back to shopping papers. I don't know. Maybe a novel? I could write this as a novel. They couldn't burst through my door then, could they? I mean, who'd believe it?"

Bolan couldn't help but smile.

A few hours later, he visited Elena's room in the hospital block. She started to well up as she tried to thank Bolan for what he had done. It was all the soldier could do to stop her. It was just another day's work.

"So how're you holding up?" he asked Elena, hoping to change the subject, and pointing to the cast that extended from wrist to neck and across her chest and the bandages covering her hands.

"I'm okay." She shrugged, and then winced as she regretted the movement. "If this is the worst I came out of this with, then it's not so bad, I guess. I should get something for being so stupid in the first place," she added bitterly.

"Everyone makes mistakes," Bolan's tone was mild, but then it grew serious. "But there were some serious things at stake here. Ricke had connections that went deeper than a crackpot philosophy and a need to gather cash. This situation nearly cost you your life, certainly your sanity, and maybe it could have cost a whole lot for the country, as well."

"All I can say is that grief does funny things to people," Elena said sadly.

Bolan smiled. "I realize that, Elena. More than you

can ever know. What's important now is how you can move on from here."

They said their goodbyes and Bolan strode out to the tarmac, breathing in the humid, sea-salty air.

An exploitative cult had been disbanded and a young woman had her life back—along with anyone else who might have fallen prey to Ricke's twisted evangelism. A power-hungry man was dead, and the nation's secrets were safe once again. At least for now.

The Executioner had been in this game long enough to know that there would always be greedy, unscrupulous people willing to take advantage of the vulnerable for their own gains. And there would always be those who sought to undermine America's security and prosperity.

Bolan's job was to keep fighting.

* * * * *

The Executioner

Don Pendleton's

POINT BLANK

Mafia Massacre

Four deputy US marshals are slaughtered with the witness they're guarding, a former Mafia member set to testify. When it's revealed the hit came from a powerful crime family, Mack Bolan decides it's time to stop the bloodshed at its source.

In Italy, Bolan learns trouble has already begun—the Mafia is intent on murdering the witness's entire family. With local law enforcement on the Mafia's payroll and spies everywhere, infiltrating the family is nearly impossible. The Mafia may have home advantage, but the Executioner won't stop until he blows their house down.

GOLD EAGLE®

Available December 2014
wherever books and ebooks are sold.

The Executioner

Don Pendleton's

SAVAGE DEADLOCK

No Man's Land

A missing US nuclear scientist resurfaces as a member of a guerrilla women's rights organization in Pakistan, raising all kinds of alarms in Washington and gaining the attention of rebel fighters.

Mack Bolan is tasked with extracting the woman and getting her Stateside, even if she doesn't want to go. But as the rebels close in and the guerrilla group realizes it's weaker than the trained fighters, Bolan and a handful of allies are forced to join the battle. Their team might be small, but the Executioner has might on his side.

GOLD EAGLE®

Available January 2015
wherever books and ebooks are sold.

GEX434

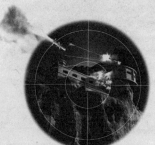